# THE REBOUND RESCUE

## DISASTER CITY SEARCH AND RESCUE, BOOK #2

### JO GRAFFORD

ISBN: 978-1-944794-52-1

# ACKNOWLEDGMENTS

Thank you so much to my wonderful beta readers — Mahasani, J. Sherlock, and Auntie Em. I also want to thank my completely amazing editor, Cathleen Weaver. Lastly, I want to give a shout-out to my Cuppa Jo Readers on Facebook for reading and loving my books!

Join Cuppa Jo Readers at https://www.facebook.

com/groups/CuppaJoReaders for sneak peeks, cover reveals, book launches, birthday parties, giveaways, and more!

## Free Book!

Also, visit www.JoGrafford.com to sign up for Jo's New Release Newsletter and receive your FREE copy of a festive short story — **Lawfully Courageous**.

## ABOUT THIS SERIES

Step into the world of Disaster City Search and Rescue, where officers, firefighters, military, and medics, train and work alongside each other with the dogs they love, to do the most dangerous job of all — help lost and injured victims find their way home.

## CHAPTER 1: THE FALL

### JETT

"Um...wow! He's hot!"

It was the beginning of March, when the annual Botany Festival at the Sam Houston National Forest was in full swing. That meant non-stop field trips from nearly every high school and college in a hundred-mile radius. Which also meant a non-stop parade of gushing, drooling female students on the forest's biking trails, hikes, and wildlife tours...

"Yep. Smoking hot!"

Forest ranger Jett Channing pretended he hadn't heard the hissing whispers between the two teens standing closest to him on his first guided tour of the morning. As a retired bodybuilding champion, he was accustomed to all the fan-girling over the size of his pecs and biceps. Normally, it didn't phase him. But ever since his way-too-public breakup a month earlier with the runner-up Miss Texas, comments like those had put him on edge.

Lately, he'd found himself longing to get away from it all — the constant attention, gossip, and headlines. And the flirting, especially the flirting. He was taking a break from the dating scene right now to clear his head and give his heart time to mend. Mending and moving on, however, would be a lot easier without the constant reminders of his recent breakup all over the news and social blogs. What he wouldn't give to be treated like a regular guy, for once!

As he approached the two-year anniversary of his service as a forest ranger, he was disappointed that the whole celebrity spotlight thing hadn't yet dimmed. Though he'd griped about it a few times to his superiors, they'd laughed it off, claiming Jett Channing's name and reputation was good for business. It kept their tours full and the rave reviews pouring in to their website.

"So, Jett," one of the teens cooed, batting her masquera-drenched lashes at him, "tell us why you decided to become a ranger."

At least that was one topic he was comfortable discussing. He just wished the slender dark-eyed hiker looked half as interested in his answer as she did his physique.

"I guess it's in my blood." He arched a brow at her and swallowed a chuckle when she audibly caught her breath and pressed a hand to her heart. Seriously, if botany didn't work out for this kid, she could always take a stab at theater. "I've been an outdoor kind of guy all my life. My dad made sure of that, teaching me how to hunt and fish at an early age, but it's more than that. My family descended from the Atakapa tribe that settled and hunted along the Sabine River. We've been close to the land for centuries, so becoming a forest ranger only made sense." For a second career, that is. His first love had been strength building.

"Oh, my gawsh! You're an Indian?" The teen batted her lashes again, looking utterly entranced.

"One of the first Americans, yes." That was the term he preferred, considering the term Indian was based on an ancient explorer's mistaken assumption that he'd sailed all the way to India instead of bumping into the New World. "Our tribe's totem is the panther." He was currently working very hard behind the scenes on behalf of the combined Atakapa-Ishak people to apply for recognition as an official tribe.

"Cool!" Her gaze dropped once more from his face to his bicep, where his tat of a black panther was peeking out from beneath his short-sleeved khaki uniform shirt.

Jett hid a grimace, relieved that their short water break was almost over. He mentally reviewed the remaining two miles or so of trail they had left and considered a detour that would require them to take on some steeper terrain. Maybe if he gave his current bevy of hikers a real challenge, the girls would be too busy climbing and sweating to pay him so much attention.

"Hey ya there, Jett!" Tess Wheeler, the manager of their ranger crew, jogged in their direction. She was a retired National Guard officer in her mid-fifties, a dyed blonde with a leathery tan from so much exposure to the sun. Usually, her wide mouth was bowed in a grin, but not this morning. Alarm glinted deep in her hazel eyes. She approached him and laid a hand on his forearm.

Pulling him aside from the teens, she stepped in close and lowered her voice. "We have a situation."

"Oh?" His girl problems dissipated as his senses kicked into high alert.

"Some research scientist wandered off down near those caverns, trying to track down a rare flower she claims is growing in the area."

"What happened?" He clenched his jaw, not liking the sound of where their conversation was heading.

"Not sure yet. Brad radioed it in on his walkie. Best we can piece together is, she slipped down a pretty steep incline. Now she's stranded on a ledge."

"Ah." He knew what that meant. "You want me to rappel down after her." Rock climbing was one of his many hobbies.

"If you're willing."

"Of course I'm willing. Tell me what you know." This was real work. Something that would require strength and skill. Something that could save a life. The burst of excitement he felt at getting out of the rest of his current tour assignment almost made him feel guilty. Teaching students about the forest was important, too. It just didn't quite hold the thrill of an emergency rescue operation.

Tess's mouth tightened as she glanced furtively at the curious teens who were watching her and Jett intently. "It's been a busy morning, I'm afraid. Both search and rescue teams on duty were sent out in the past hour to help track down students who got sepa-rated from the main huddle. Probably no real emer-gencies there. Problem is, it'll take a good bit of time to get either team back to send over to the caverns, and Brad is worried the scientist might not have that long. She appears dizzy and disoriented. He's with her now." Tess dangled her keys beneath Jett's nose. "My truck is just over the next ridge. Why don't you scram while I take over your tour?"

Jett nodded, swiped the keys, and took off running. If the situation hadn't been so serious, he might have found the disappointed sighs of the female hikers he was leaving behind to be humorous. *Ah, well.* They'd soon discover they were in good hands with their replacement tour guide. Tess knew the forest like the back of her hand — every nook and cranny, every unexpected detail, including the coveted eagles nest a few hills over.

He reached the truck and took off, spinning sand. The caverns were about five miles away, and the road would not take him all the way there. The last quarter mile or so would have to be made on foot.

While he drove, Jett used the voice-activated feature on the dashboard system of Tess's government vehicle to call Brad. "How's our wandering scientist faring?"

"She's hanging in there, but you need to hurry." Brad dropped his voice. "I think she hit her head. She's mumbling to herself and crying a little."

"You found a place to anchor the rope for me?"

"Is the sky blue?"

Jett glanced briefly up at the sky. "For now."

"I've got you all set up." Brad let out a heavy huff of air. "If it weren't for this bum knee of mine, I'd have already gone down after her, myself."

"No need," Jett assured quickly. "I'll be there in two minutes tops." He reached the pull-out area on the side of the road that overlooked the caverns, braked, and leaped from the truck. As a precaution, he grabbed Tess's extra crevasse rescue kit from the back of the truck. Wouldn't hurt to have an additional harness to strap around the stranded hiker. Depending on what shape she was in when he reached her, she might not prove much help in her own rescue.

Then Jett took off at a run through the tall sycamore, oak, and ash trees. He was more grateful than ever for the park's skilled landscaping crew. They had done a tremendous job of clearing the deadwood and underbrush from around the most toured areas of the forest throughout the winter months. Not only was a well-kept forest a deterrent to forest fires, it made things a lot easier on the hikers or, in this case, a single runner.

Jett's all-terrain boots had set him back several hundred dollars, but they were worth every penny when it came time to trek through the forest. Being able to afford custom footwear was one of the perks of his last career, which had left him with a few sizable portfolios of endorsement earnings and championship winnings.

He crested the final hill to reach the caverns, and Brad's worried features came into view. The middle-aged security guard straightened from his crouch over the short metal railing and pushed back his cap to give Jett a satisfied nod. The brown hair curling out from beneath his cap was streaked with silver. "You sure did make it in record time. Did you run the entire way?"

"Something like that." Jett joined him at the rail and sent a light punch to his shoulder. "Guess our stranded scientist didn't see the signs." He raised his brows at Brad. There weren't many cliffs or other steep inclines in this part of the forest. The few they had, however, were clearly marked with warning signs — like this one. He leaned over the railing to assess how far down the woman had fallen.

A pair of slightly glazed-over blue eyes stared back at him — very beautiful blue eyes with a beseeching cast to them. Definitely not what Jett had been expecting when Tess had described her as a research scientist. The white lab coat, protection goggles, and test tubes his mind had conjured up weren't even close to the reality. Nope. This woman had *experienced hiker* written all over her, from her smoothly braided long red hair to her sturdy boots, navy vest, and olive cargo shorts.

She swayed dizzily and muttered something that sounded like "Thank, God."

"I'm Jett Channing, and I'm here to help you," he called down to her. "What's your name?" He swiftly locked himself onto the ropes with his carabiners. Since she seemed lucid enough, he planned to keep her talking. He wanted her to focus on him instead of the steep drop-off in front of her.

"Gwenyth Moore," she supplied in a rueful tone. "All-around idiot extraordinaire, as it turns out."

Her fall certainly hadn't erased her sense of humor. That was a good sign. Grinning, Jett swung himself easily over the guard rail and started his descent. It was only about twenty feet, but he didn't want to move too quickly and inadvertently rain down a bunch of pebbles and debris onto her.

"Falling doesn't make you an idiot," he assured, hoping to keep Gwenyth talking. "Everyone makes mistakes."

She gave a breathy chuckle. "Oh, this silly fall is nothing compared to some of the other things I've done." There was a sobbing hitch to her voice. "As it turns out, the last three years of my life have been one gigantic mistake."

"Is that so?" Jett had no idea what the woman was talking about and wasn't in a hurry to find out, but he still needed to keep her talking. Another glance down proved the narrow ledge was slanted more downward than he'd originally estimated. It was a miracle the woman hadn't already plunged over the edge.

So much for worrying about raining pebbles! He needed to get down there and fast! He let the rope out more quickly and reached her in three large bounds. Since there was very little room on the ledge, he ended up straddling Gwenyth's legs, which were bent like a hairpin and trembling from the effort to hold herself up against the steep hillside.

His blood ran cold at the realization that it was her hand tangled in the vine above her head and the strength in her own legs that had kept her from plunging over the side, a strength that was fast waning according to how badly she was shaking. The other thing that quickly became apparent was that the wrist lying limply in her lap was broken.

"Here, let's get you in the harness." Sympathy and admiration laced his voice. He couldn't help being impressed by her obvious grit and determination to survive.

"Maybe you could help me stand first?" she squeaked. Her face was alarmingly pale beneath a light sprinkling of freckles. "I've been sitting for what feels like hours on shards of glass."

"Glass!" He gently maneuvered the woman to her feet and held her steady while she brushed at her backside. Sure enough, a tinkling sound met his ears as a piece of glass dropped to the ledge.

"My eyeglasses," she explained in a dry voice. "I'm not complaining, though. I'm pretty sure the pain was the only thing keeping me from passing out." She swayed forward, and he caught her against his chest. "Good golly! Why are there two of you?"

He swiftly buckled her into the extra harness and straightened, frowning down into her face. "Probably because you have a concussion. Here." He lifted her arm with the broken wrist and drew it around his neck. "Why don't you pretend I'm a tree for the next sixty seconds or so? You're going to need to hang on as tightly as you can for this next part."

She nodded and drew her other arm around his neck. "Believe me, it's not the first time I've been accused of being a tree hugger." With those words, she burst into tears and buried her face against his shoulder.

Not knowing what he'd said to set her off, Jett clicked on an extra carabiner for good measure to make sure their two harnesses were securely linked. Then he made the rally sign over his head to indicate to Brad they were ready to be pulled back up.

In the promised minute, Jett stepped with Gwenyth over the top of the railing, back onto safe ground.

Brad took one look at Gwenyth's bedraggled condition while Jett was releasing her from the harness. "I'll call an ambulance."

She sagged against Jett, all dusty and spent. Her elbows and knees were scraped, and her eyelids kept drifting closed.

"Hey, stay with me, Gwenyth."

"I know, I know," she muttered, forcing her lids open again.

Jett hooked an arm around her middle to hold her upright while he glanced over the top of her head at Brad. "I think I'll drive her." He hated the idea of her having to wait another half hour or more for the paramedics to arrive, when he could have her at the nearest hospital in less time than that. "Want to ride shotgun?"

Brad straightened his black cap uncertainly. "Normally I'd not think twice about saying yes, but we're pretty shorthanded around here today. How badly do you need me?"

Jett frowned. "Unfortunately, the visitors center is in the opposite direction of the hospital."

"That's okay." Brad's expression cleared. "I may not be able to scale cliffs these days like you younger fellows, but there isn't anything wrong with my trotting abilities."

"Alright, then." Unfortunately, Gwenyth's trotting abilities seemed to be long gone. Jett gently lifted her in his arms and carried her toward the truck.

Brad followed. The moment they reached the truck, Brad dug in a cooler strapped inside the bed and came up with a bottle of chilled water. "Here." He uncapped it and handed it to Gwenyth. "Drink."

Her fingers trembled, but she complied while Jett got her strapped into a seatbelt. After she took a few sips, she gave a violent shiver. "It's so c-cold," she mumbled, tipping her head against the seat rest.

"She's going into shock." Jett's jaw tightened, glancing wildly around the back seat of the truck. "Do you see any blankets around here?"

Brad shook his head, and a quick search proved fruitless.

"The heater it is." Jett rolled his eyes, knowing he'd be sweating bullets in no time. A heavily muscled chap like himself had plenty of natural insulation. He tended to get hot easily, but their wounded hiker's needs would have to come first.

"Godspeed!" Brad gave him a mock salute as Jett leaped into the driver's seat and started the engine.

As he nosed Tess's truck onto the road that would lead them to the interstate, Jett glanced over at Gwenyth. To his alarm, her eyes were closed again. Her broken right wrist was resting in her lap.

*No!* The first taste of panic filled his mouth. Maybe he should have waited for an ambulance, after all. It wasn't as if he was trained in much more than basic first aide.

"Gwenyth?" he asked sharply. "You still with me over there?"

"Not g-going anywhere." This time she spoke through gritted teeth.

Again, he was struck by her spunk and obvious grasp on her humor. She was turning out to be one of the strongest people he'd ever encountered. He wracked his brain for a topic of conversation that would hold her interest enough to slice through her pain and increasing tendrils of shock.

"You said something earlier about the last three years of your life being one big mistake." *Man!* He felt like a cad for bringing it up. But if it kept her conscious long enough to get her to the hospital... "What did you mean by that?"

To his horror, tears started to slide down her pale, dusty cheeks, leaving muddy rivulets. "My b-boyfriend of three years just d-ditched me for a supermodel."

Jett notched up the heater another few degrees as he drove to the freeway intersection and cruised down the entrance ramp. "When?" he demanded, surprised at how incensed he felt on Gwenyth's behalf.

"Yesterday. Th-that's why I came here to g-go camping last night. I didn't want to b-be alone."

*Smart girl!* His heart twisted in sympathy. After going through a bad breakup of his own a month ago, he was well acquainted with those kinds of feelings. It was best not to be alone in the dark with those emotions for too long. They could eat you alive from the inside out — all the hurt, the self doubt, the continuous questioning about what you might have, or should have, done differently to prevent it from coming to this. Playing the inner blame game was like fighting a vicious beast, and it was a fight that nobody ever came out a winner of.

"My manager said you're a research scientist."

Gwenyth's lips quirked despite her tears. "The very best," she boasted in a damp but laughing tone.

Jett was utterly charmed. He couldn't remember the last time he'd enjoyed being in the presence of any female this much. Gwenyth Moore was delightfully funny, intelligent, and refreshingly without guile. More importantly, her shaking was subsiding, and her voice was sounding more clear. That was good for both of them, because the temperature inside the cab had risen to a scalding eighty degrees. Jett was about ready to have a heatstroke.

"I might've leaned too far over that ledge and taken a tumble, but I managed to harvest a rare flower." She patted the upper pocket of her navy vest. "Roots and all."

He shook his head. "You're something else! You know that?"

To his dismay, her striking blue eyes filled with tears again. "Just not pretty enough or interesting enough to hold Gator John's attention."

Jett straightened in his seat, wondering if he'd heard right. "Are you referring to the guy who stars in that bayou show?" The man's show was a bit on the cheesy side, but it pulled in some pretty high ratings. The guy was like a super hero to most of the elementary school kids who signed up for the Sam Houston National Forest tours.

"Yes, *that* Gator John," Gwenyth affirmed bitterly. "We both love science and animals...and the outdoors. He even had me on his show a few times as his guest. It truly seemed like a match made in heaven. Until he met Yasmin Guerra."

Jett blinked. He'd heard the name. She was a big-time supermodel. Big-time, as in big contracts and big money.

"A lowly research scientist just can't compete with that kind of glitter and glam."

*Ouch!* Jett's sympathy-meter soared another few

notches. He and Gwenyth were turning out to have an awful lot in common, emphasis on the awful. His breakup with Holland Dadashi had been splashed across more headlines than he could keep track of. In hindsight, he suspected she'd merely used his celebrity status in the attempt to boost her own. The moment she'd come in second in the Miss Texas vote, it had been over between them. She'd bitterly accused him of being a has-been who was more of a liability than an asset to her career as a rising actress.

"I'm sorry." Jett reached for Gwenyth's one good hand and squeezed it. "Gator John must have taken a bite from one too many rabid alligators or something, because I say he was a fool to give you up." He meant it, too. He'd only known Gwenyth Moore for less than an hour, and already he was interested in getting to know her better.

"You're just saying that to make me feel better." Her eyes drifted closed again.

He squeezed her hand. "Is it working?" To his relief, the outline of the hospital and its adjoining parking garage materialized against the Houston skyline.

In less than five minutes, he was braking in front of the emergency room. Two medics were exiting the sliding glass doors with an empty stretcher rolling between them.

Jett waved them over. "A little help, please?"

## CHAPTER 2: HER HERO

### GWENYTH

The next half hour or so passed in a blur as Gwenyth's vitals were taken by the ER nurse, and the physician on duty made his way over to examine her.

"I'm Dr. Frank. The fellow who drove you here said you took quite a tumble."

She squinted at him, feeling dizzy as he shone a penlight in her eyes to check for dilation. "Unless I hit my head harder than I think I did, it was Jett Channing." The famous bodybuilder had been a hundred more shades of gorgeous up close than he'd ever been on T.V., but she'd been too injured to appreciate that fact.

"The one and only," Dr. Frank affirmed cheerfully. "It's my lucky day, getting to meet two celebrities back-to-back like this. Not so lucky for you, I suppose."

*Me? A celebrity?* Who in the heck did he think she was?

He directed the nurse to put her on an I.V. drip. It buoyed her strength and made her feel almost back to normal within minutes. And, joy of joys, they packed her in layer after layer of heated blankets while they set her wrist in a cast.

"It's a simple fracture. You're very fortunate, Dr. Moore."

Her gaze flickered from the cast to the kind face of the attending physician. "You know who I am?"

"Do I!" He gave a delighted chuckle. "I own both your books on herbal treatments. If they didn't have the misfortune to be sitting at home right now on my bookshelf, I'd probably have the poor manners to ask you to autograph them for me — I.V., cast, and all."

*Ah.* So *that's* why he'd called her a celebrity. He was just being nice. She smiled. "If you want, I could drop back by here in a few days to make that happen."

"I want." His voice was admiring but matter-of-fact as he fished in the pocket of his white coat for a business card. He set it on the portable silver night-stand next to her hospital bed. "Here's my card. You're welcome to take it with you when you check out."

"Thank you." She frowned thoughtfully at him. "How soon can I leave?" She'd have to call a cab, since her car was back at the Sam Houston National Forest camping grounds.

He leaned over her bed to pat her good hand. "I'm afraid your concussion has earned you an overnight stay for observation. We're working on getting an inpatient room set up for you."

"No, please!" she protested. "I don't want to say overnight." She hated hospitals and their antiseptic smells. "Are there any other options?" *Please say yes!*

"Only if you have someone who can keep an eye on you overnight." His smile was replaced with a look of concern. "It's vitally important that someone else be there to wake you now and then to ensure your symptoms aren't getting worse, also to make sure you're able to sleep and wake normally." He grimaced. "I don't mean to pry, Dr. Moore, but do you have any family or friends who can stay the night with you?"

"I, ah..." *No, not exactly.* "Of course I do," she lied, her mind racing over the possibilities. Unfortunately, she was relatively new in town, only recently having arrived to accept the coveted position of department chair and lead research scientist at the College of Science & Engineering at Sam Houston State University. The only person she'd actually introduced herself to was the nice little widow she'd met the other day outside the condominium next to hers. Then again, Gwenyth could also simply return to the camping site where she was guaranteed to be surrounded by lots of other hikers and campers.

"Good." Dr. Frank nodded in satisfaction. "I'll get your discharge papers ready, then. I'd still like to keep you another hour for observation, just to be safe. Thanks to Mr. Channing, you didn't go all the way into shock, but you certainly were borderline when you arrived."

Gwenyth glanced down at her vest, hoping her wallet and keys were still intact, not to mention the precious plant she'd harvested. To her shock, her vest was missing. In fact, all her clothes were missing. She was wearing a white hospital gown. "My vest!" she gasped, moving her head frantically back and forth to take in the small curtained-off space. "My things! Where are they?"

"Whoa, there, tiger!" Dr. Frank held up a hand. "I believe Mr. Channing retained possession of your belongings. He said something about needing to preserve a plant you found in the forest."

Gwenyth was so relieved that a fresh round of tears formed in her eyes. "Where is he?" she choked. If that blasted muscle-bound man had managed to save her precious flower, she would literally kiss his feet the next time she saw him.

"In the waiting room. I can go get him, if you'd like."

"Yes, please." She nodded her head and immediately regretted the movement when a slice of pain shot through her temples.

"Easy there, Dr. Moore." The doctor winked at her. "You're going to want to take things slow for the next few days. I'm prescribing rest, more rest, a bottle of Tylenol for the pain, and plenty of fluids."

"Aye, aye, doc." Gwenyth raised her cast in a mock salute, and immediately regretted that movement, as well. Every inch of her body hurt. It felt like there were scrapes on top of her scrapes and bruises on top of her bruises.

He disappeared beyond the curtain. Minutes later, the curtains slowly parted. "Uh, Dr. Moore? Is it okay if I come in?"

The outline of Jett Channing's hulking figure appeared on the other side of the curtain. From the small handful of fabric he'd pulled aside, she could see his face was carefully averted. *Good heavens!* The guy was so crazy good looking it nearly took her breath away. He was built, too, all tanned and ripped. Probably had women swooning all over him all the time, which meant she needed to be super careful not to act like that. No doubt he was sick and tired of it.

"Only if you're prepared to be wowed out by my cool hospital gown and pretty white cast," she joked, knowing she must look positively atrocious. That had to be a novel experience for Jett — being in the same room with a woman who didn't look like red carpet material. Gwenyth longed for a shower and a fresh change of clothing.

He stepped inside, shaking his head. "You really are something else, Dr. Moore—"

*Oh, sheesh! Seriously?* "You can drop the title, already." She held up her good hand. "It's clear you stumbled across my university I.D."

He looked sheepish. "I'm sorry. I kinda needed it to get you checked in and all."

"Well, I'm not sorry," she retorted bluntly. "Not one bit. I'm wildly grateful for everything you've done for me today. Considering the fact that I'm a horrible cook and possess no crafting and gift making abilities, I have no idea how I'm ever going to thank you. That is, unless, you're willing to settle for coffee or ice cream." She smiled at him, feeling shy. "Or dinner?" *Good heavens!* What had gotten into her? It was like she was asking the guy on a date or something.

"Just doing my job, ma'am." He inclined his head at her.

*Ma'am?* "Gwenyth," she corrected firmly. "Just Gwenyth, please. I'm sorry, but there's just no going back to doctor or ma'am after you've seen a woman in her hospital gown."

He threw back his head and laughed. "As they like to say in the deep south, you're a hot mess." The term was accompanied by an admiring glint in his dark eyes that took the sting out of the insult.

"I'm originally from the great Down Under. New Zealand, actually." She motioned at the black swivel stool Dr. Frank had recently vacated. "My parents moved here when I was a small kid, found jobs, applied for citizenship, and stayed."

"In Texas?" He took a seat on the stool.

She was greatly relieved to see her vest draped neatly over one of his massive forearms. "Yep. In the great nation of Texas," she teased. "Pasadena, to be exact." Living in a bay town was how she'd met Gator John. He was forever filming his shows on the coastline near the Louisiana and Texas border.

"Well, don't you sound like a regular cowgirl?" His voice was approving.

"Yeah, well, I'm missing my Stetson, so it must be the braids," she quipped, fingering the one loosely woven plait that was draped over her shoulder. Call her desperate, but she was intent on making a friend of Jett Channing and fast. He'd been kind enough to bring her to the hospital, which she knew was above and beyond the call of duty, when he could have just as easily called an ambulance and sent her on her way. Maybe he'd be kind enough to drive her back to the campgrounds, too.

Jett made a huffing sound. "More like the stubborn streak a mile wide running straight down between your pretty eyes."

Again, his compliment-encased insult bore no

sting. "Me? Stubborn?" She pressed her hand to her chest, trying to look innocent.

"Very, very stubborn, Professor Moore."

She stuck her tongue out at him. "What is it with you and titles?" *Come on!* First doctor, then ma'am, and now professor.

"Hey!" He held up both hands, palms facing her. "Respect, alright? Guess I haven't run into too many women brandishing PhDs." He lowered his large hands to his knees. "It's a novel experience."

"I hope that's a good thing, despite the unfortunate circumstances that caused our paths to cross today." She hoped she didn't sound as anxious as she felt.

"I'm here, aren't I?" He gave her a curiously intent look that was accompanied by a quizzical smile.

She felt a blush heat her cheeks. All her promises to herself from earlier faded. She was seriously close to swooning beneath all that dark-eyed, admiring intensity. "Well, since I've utterly failed to scare you off with my dusty braids and the whole damsel-in-distress thing, I was hoping to ask for one last favor."

To her surprise, his expression grew shuttered, and he glanced away.

*What now? Did I say something wrong?* She gave a silent sigh and plowed onward. "I want you to help break me out of here, okay?"

A chuckle escaped him, and his dark gaze

returned to hers. "You're not a prisoner here, you know. When Dr. Frank fetched me from the waiting room, he claimed he was releasing you within the hour."

She glanced around the curtained-off bay, to ensure they were still alone, and lowered her voice to barely above a whisper. "Only because I lied."

"About?" he prodded, wrinkling his dark brows at her.

"About having someone to keep an eye on me tonight." She paused. "Because of the concussion," she added, biting her lower lip in embarrassment. "The truth is, I'm new in town. The only person I've met so far is a widow lady in the condo next door and a couple of coworkers. So..." this time she was the one who glanced away, "I was really hoping you would be so kind as to drive me back to the campsite where I can at least be around plenty of other campers for the evening."

"Absolutely not!" He sounded so horrified that she glanced up in surprise.

"Why? What does it matter to you if I spring this joint?" she demanded irritably. If Jett dared to blow her cover story with Dr. Frank and ended up landing her here in the hospital overnight, she was seriously going to find something to throw at him. "We barely know each other."

"Whatever," he snapped. "I'm only the guy who scraped you off a ledge in the park and drove you to the hospital, so you didn't have to wait for an ambulance." There was no mistaking the sarcasm in his voice...or the accusation.

"Aw, are you trying to say we're friends now, Jett?"

"Kinda. Maybe." He threw up his hands with an exasperated sound. "Listen, I feel responsible for you, okay?"

"Wow!" She scowled at him. "If that means you're going to leave me stuck in this hospital overnight, let me lay it out real simple for you. Our budding friendship will not survive this."

"Ouch! That hurts." He glared at her. "A few minutes ago, I thought we were getting close to going out for coffee or ice cream together."

The fact that Jett Channing — *the* Jett Channing — had just used the words "we" and "going out" in the same sentence, did not make her feel any less like crying. "You should be glad I don't have an ice cream cone in my hand right now. I'd probably throw it at you."

He studied her closely for several long moments. "You really don't like hospitals, huh?" His tone was milder than before.

"Not even a little." To her mortification, a lone tear slipped down her cheek. "What brought my family all the way from New Zealand to Texas was the cancer treatment center at MD Anderson."

"I'm sorry." He looked and sounded grave. "One of your parents had cancer?"

She shook her head. "It was a rare tumor located along my spinal cord. Very serious but treatable. I was one of the lucky kids who got to go home, but only after many, many, many months in the hospital."

"I see." He was silent for so long that she started to grow sleepy again.

She tried and failed to suppress a yawn.

"Okay," he finally said, swiveling on the stool to face her squarely. "If I spring you out of here, what's in it for me?"

She struggled to push back the webs of sleep that were fast closing around her brain. "Dinner before ice cream? Or after ice cream? Your choice."

"Sold." He stood abruptly to drape her vest on the bed railing. "But I'm not taking you back to the campgrounds, no matter how many ugly names you call me inside your head or how many things you find to throw at me." He shook a finger beneath her nose when she started to splutter. "Lucky for you, I'm on call tonight, which means I'll have the cabin behind the visitors center all to myself. You can stay there, while I go gather your things. Where did you say you pitched your tent?"

"The Double Lake Recreation Area. Lot 10." She reached for the car keys inside her vest pocket. "I drive a silver Porsche, if you care to fetch that, too."

He reached for the keys. "Who drives a Porsche to a campground?"

"Me," she said evenly, "since it's the only car I own. What's with the anti-Porsche sentiment?"

"Nothing." He shook his head. "It's just not the usual set of wheels for an outdoorsy type person."

*Now I'm the outdoorsy type?* Gwenyth hardly knew what to say to that. It tickled her to no end, however, that Jett seemed to be trying to figure her out. She loved how she'd managed to keep him guessing so far.

With another head-shake, he reached behind her and produced her cargo shorts, socks, and hiking boots. "Think you can manage to get these back on?"

"Or die trying," she assured grimly, struggling to sit up. The movement elicited a huff of pain from her. Lord help her, but every cell in her body was screaming.

He watched her in concern for a moment longer before silently taking his leave of her.

A nurse appeared a few minutes later to remove the I.V.

"Thank you," Gwenyth mumbled. She was already dressed from the waist down. "Do you think you could help a girl out, here?" There were certain clasps and buttons that were going to be tricky to manage with one hand.

"Sure!" the nurse declared cheerfully. "Or I could go fetch that handsome man of yours."

"What? Oh, no! We're not, that is...I'm sure you and I can muddle through the dressing stuff just fine." Gwenyth blushed to realize the nurse had presumed she and Jett were together, as in *together* together.

"So how did the two of you meet?" The nurse helped her pull on her shirt and vest with quick, efficient movements.

Gwenyth was way too sore and tired to concoct anything, so she opted for the truth. "I fell down an incline and got stranded on a ledge in the park. Jett rescued me and brought me here."

"Wow! A real-life hero," the nurse breathed.

"Total hero material," Gwenyth agreed. He had the whole knight in shining armor thing nailed to the absolute wall.

The gleeful light in the nurse's eyes made Gwenyth wonder if the woman would be tweeting about her and Jett as soon as they left the ER together. Most folks simply did not understand the importance of privacy when it came to dealing with celebrities. She should probably warn Jett.

The curtains parted shortly after she was dressed, and her hero reappeared, pushing a wheelchair. He waggled his eyebrows at her and motioned toward the black leather seat. "Your chariot awaits, my lady."

She laughed. "You sure do know how to show a girl a good time."

"What can I say?" He spread his hands. "Got a reputation to protect."

She winced as she slid to her feet and would have pitched forward if it wasn't for his quick lunge in her direction.

"Guess you weren't kidding about dying while trying," he grumbled, pivoting with her to sit her down in the wheelchair.

The nurse returned with the discharge paper-work. Gwenyth signed everything while hardly looking at it, though Jett asked a few questions about the forms.

Only when they approached his black work truck with the magnetic national forest sign on the door did she breathe freely. "We did it!" she crowed softly.

"By we, you mean it was mostly me," Jett corrected smugly. He helped her climb into the cab, then leaned over her to buckle the seatbelt. "But don't worry, I fully intend to collect my dinner and ice cream."

"Jett Channing?" a female voice trilled.

A flash of bulbs made Gwenyth squint and see stars for several seconds. *Great! Just great!* She'd forgotten all about warning Jett, and now it looked as if the paparazzi had found them.

"Here." He removed his uniform cap and placed it on her head. It was too big for her, so it was easy for him to pull it low over her eyes. "Sorry about this, but don't worry. This is not my first rodeo. There's only two of them, a cameraman and a reporter, so I should have you out of here in no time."

Maybe it was the head injury making her thoughts fuzzy again; but, unless Gwenyth was mistaken, Jett was actually apologizing to *her* about the paparazzi instead of blaming her for their presence.

## CHAPTER 3: JUST FRIENDS

### JETT

Jett had sort of fudged about being on call at the national forest that evening. He'd actually been on call two nights ago, but it wouldn't take long to jimmy his schedule with a few rangers and get put on duty again for the night.

He might even be able to get his work schedule switched over the phone during their ride back to the Sam Houston National Forest, since Gwenyth fell asleep before they exited the hospital parking lot.

Keeping an eye on her for the night was only something any decent friend would do, and Gwenyth was fast becoming exactly that — a friend. Certainly nothing more. He was on a self-imposed dating diet, a fact that had somehow made the news. Grimacing at the memory, he shot a sideways glance in Gwenyth's direction. Something told him that the gossip rags would have plenty to say about the supposed end to his girlfriend diet when pictures of him and his sleeping beauty over there in the passenger seat made headlines later this evening.

Movement in the side-view mirrors alerted him to the fact they were being followed. It was a dark SUV with tinted windows. A figure leaned out the passenger window, and a camera flashed, verifying it was a reporter — most likely the same one they'd encountered in the parking lot.

With a growl of irritation, Jett cut it close at the next red light and hung a left. He slowed and watched as the driver of the SUV attempted to run the light, but oncoming traffic forced her to jam on her brakes.

*Too easy!* Jett gunned the truck motor and took off. He still wasn't free and clear just yet. Most reporters he knew had friends. No doubt this woman was already calling in favors. He stuck to alleys and side streets downtown, which forced him to avoid the freeway and take the long way back to work. He didn't mind, though. Dr. Gwenyth Moore was turning out to be well worth the effort.

He continued to steal glances at her while she slept. Though she wasn't anything like the other women he'd dated — not that they were dating — she had an appeal that was all her own. Her red hair and creamy skin wasn't exactly hard on the eyes any more than her faint New Zealand accent was hard on the ears. Her oval features possessed the classic lines and curves he'd known other women to undergo surgery to achieve. However, he couldn't detect any tiny, obscure scar lines at her temples that would suggest surgery.

From what he could tell, his new professor friend was entirely genuine, right down to her clumsiness near cliffs and her rabid fear of hospitals. Man, but he'd be lying to himself if he didn't admit she was appealing — the whole package. If he was in the market for a girlfriend, that is. Which he wasn't...

Jett's smugness at outmaneuvering the paparazzi quickly disappeared at the sight of three news channel vans in the parking lot of the visitors center.

*Of all the rotten—* With a grunt of irritation, he avoided the turn-in to the parking lot and kept on driving. *What to do... What to do...* At the next inter-section, there were signs pointing to the various hiking trails and fishing areas as well as the three campgrounds. He nosed Tess's truck in the direction of The Double Lake Recreation Area.

Looked like Gwenyth was going to get her wish to return to her tent, after all. "Guess it's a good thing I didn't get around to changing my work schedule just yet," he muttered beneath his breath.

"Did you say something?" The woman in ques-tion yawned and stretched, which led to a wince and a moan.

"I did. Was talking to myself, but now that you're awake..." He pulled the truck up to Lot 10. Even if he hadn't seen the number on the sign, he would have known this was her camping unit from the flashy silver Porsche parked next to the largest navy and silver tent he'd ever laid eyes on.

He turned to her. "You seriously call this camping?" There was a waist-high, hourglass shaped smoker grill resting outside her tent, a stainless steel bonfire stove, and a portable fridge and freezer combo that was plugged in to the electrical hookup post. He couldn't begin to imagine what creature comforts were inside her tent; but, at this point, his money was on genie lamps and magic carpets.

"I'm actually not much of a camper," she admitted in a sheepish voice.

"No kidding?" He made no attempt to hide his sarcasm.

"I am, however, serious about my botany research, so camping is a necessary evil, on occasion." She squinted across the cab at him. "Good news. There's only one of you now."

"Glad to hear it." He leaned over to unbuckle her seatbelt but took his time moving back to his side of the truck, drinking in her curious gaze. What he saw behind the curiousness made his heart thud a little harder. There was admiration mixed with the curiosity, though she'd made no effort to flirt with him the entire morning or afternoon thus far. "Please assure me you have a spare pair of spectacles somewhere in that mansion of a tent there, squinty."

"I do, thankfully, but gosh! I have to ask. Are you always this charming?" She opened the passenger door with a huff of exertion.

He hurried around the truck to help her. "Only on Fridays," he assured, glancing pointedly at his watch. "Like Cinderella, all this magic," he gave an exaggerated circular wave at himself, "ends at midnight, so enjoy it while it lasts."

"Party on!" she muttered, sagging against him once more.

When it was all said and done, his diva of a research scientist had a pretty good thing going at her campsite. As he guided her closer, he could see everything was bolted down with thin, steel cables. Subtle but effective. Her tent was no exception. She actually had a portable security system rigged that required her to type in a code to disengage it.

"Alright, I'll just throw this down. I'm impressed," he admitted, as they entered her tent together. He was a tall man and had to stoop, but not as much as he expected to. It was a fairly sizable setup.

"Great!" she shot back. "I survived a risky fall and a trip to the hospital, only to faint with surprise when you finally pay me a compliment."

He chuckled and snatched back his cap and returned it to his own head as he led her deeper into her inner sanctum. The tent consisted of four small rooms. The first one was clearly designed to serve as a living room and media room with a navy, two-person reclinable lounge that could be folded when not in use. The next compartment was set up as a science lab with all sorts of equipment from microscopes to a portable cabinet with drawers to various items he didn't recognize. The third room turned out to be her bedroom, where he discovered his speculation about magic carpets hadn't been all that far off. It was a queen-sized monstrosity that extended from wall-to-wall, and it was covered in a plush duvet that boasted a Thomas Kincade-esque scene of deer grazing in the moonlight.

Jett started to lower Gwenyth to her bed but stopped when she yelped in protest. "Ew, no! I'm way too filthy to climb into bed yet. Shower first."

"How are you going to manage—?"

"I'll figure it out," she cut in. "Cleanliness is one of those non-negotiable things." She frowned and glanced across the room to where she had another set of portable shelves suspended from the ceiling.

Jett perceived it must be her closet of sorts. Or a hanging dresser? "You really need to invest in an R.V."

"On that we agree." Her voice was sunny with cheer.

"How did you get all this stuff piled into a Porsche, anyway?" There was just no way.

"I didn't. I own a light-weight collapsable trailer to haul the bigger things."

"Of course you do." Shaking his head, Jett returned Gwenyth to her living room and deposited her in her lounge while he gathered her change of clothes and a small collection of toiletries. Basically, he played the part of her valet and followed the orders she called to him through the thin canvas walls. Since she couldn't see him, Jett couldn't resist peeking inside the final and smallest room, which turned out to be a powder room, complete with an incinerator toilet. *Why am I not surprised?* He tripped on a silver bucket on his way out the door and discovered it contained the final item he'd been searching for — a rolled-up beach towel.

"Looking for skeletons?" Gwenyth inquired mischievously from the living room.

"Maybe." Jett returned to her, holding out a navy tote bag. He set it in her lap. "Make sure it has everything you need before you hit the shower, princess."

"Oh, right. Because all your charm disappears at midnight."

"Bingo." He made a shooting motion with his thumb and forefinger. It seemed to him that she was a bit steadier on her feet during the short walk to the building that housed the public restrooms and showers. For that Jett was grateful, because he didn't know what else he could do for her at this point.

After she showered and was safely returned to her tent, he ensured she was hydrated, then rustled around for something to eat. "I'm not hungry," she called sleepily from her bed. "Eating is something I'll gladly skip in lieu of a nap."

"You need to keep your strength up," he retorted, unearthing a box of granola bars.

"If I promise to put in an order for delivery, will you let me sleep?" she shot back weakly.

Throwing up his hands, Jett relented. Ordering out sounded just fine to him. "Listen, I need to return Tess's truck and run a few errands. I'll be back before dark to check on you, alright?"

"Aren't you on duty tonight?" she mumbled.

"That was the plan." He didn't bother explaining his updated plans and was glad she was too tired to ply him with any more questions. "So...do you trust me enough to give me your security code?"

"Zero one zero one zero zero."

He smiled. "Is that a science-y way of warning intruders? Binary code for *stay the heck out of my tent* or something?"

"No." Her voice was sluggish and faint this time. "It stands for January 1, 2000. The day I was declared cancer free."

Okay. That was an emotional punch in the gut — in a good way, though. Jett blew out a pent-up breath of air and shook his head. Yeah, it looked like his girl-friend diet was well and truly over. He wanted to date this woman, plain and simple.

It was way too stinking bad she was only one day past her breakup from Gator John. Those things took time to recover from. He could attest to that first-hand. It might be awhile before Gwenyth was ready to date again, and he intended to give her that time — all the time she needed. He didn't want to be her second choice or her rebound guy. He wanted to be her final choice when she made it. Her one and only.

*Oka-a-a-ay!* He had no idea where that thought had come from. It was just there, and it was real. Jogging back to Tess's truck, Jett revved the motor and took off in the direction of the visitor's center. No doubt he was going to get the scolding of his life for being gone so long, but he didn't care. He was pretty sure he'd just experienced love at first sight, or at least at first encounter — the stuff books and movies were made of.

And it wasn't made of lightning and pixie dust like he imagined it would be. It was a meeting of hearts and minds, an overwhelming admiration like he'd never felt before for another human being. But it was more than even that. Lord help him, but he was every bit as attracted to her wit and sass as he was her willowy curves and fiery hair. And those sparkling blue eyes! *Yeah.* They could sparkle back at him all day long, as far as he was concerned. No, it wasn't just one thing that attracted him to Dr. Gwenyth Moore, research scientist, professor, and self-proclaimed klutz extraordinaire. It was the whole package. Every kind, brave, open-faced, joy-for-living inch of her.

It was a few minutes past the national park's official closing time when Jett arrived back to the welcome center, but Tess Wheeler didn't look near ready to close up shop for the evening. On the other hand, she didn't look as furious as he'd anticipated, either.

"Well, look what the cat dragged in," she declared dryly, rising from her desk chair and stretching as if to relieve a kink in her back. "How is the lovely Dr. Moore?" She strode around to the front of her desk, shoved a stack of papers aside, and hiked her hip on it. "I wouldn't mind hearing your version of her escapade on our grounds, since I've been regaled by about every other version all afternoon on T.V." She lifted a remote control from her desk and aimed it at the television mounted on the wood-paneled wall in the corner of the room. "To include one very irate call from the district ranger's office in New Waverly. They wanted to remind me we have procedures to follow around here, including filing proper incident reports and the like."

Jett shot a sheepish look at the screen, not all that surprised to see his own face splashed across it. However, he cringed at the scrolling headlines across the bottom.

Former bodybuilding champion Jett
Channing rescues research

scientist after near-fatal plunge
over cliff.

Jett Channing rushes wounded hiker
to hospital.

Fall victim believed to be former
fiancée of TV Host Gator John.

Then there was all the speculation about a budding relationship between Jett and Gwenyth, along with several wisecrack attempts to pair their names together — everything from Jettyth to Gwenning to Chamoore.

Jett shuddered at the name pairings, knowing Gwenyth was going to be utterly snowed in with all this nonsense when she returned to work on Monday. "I'll have the incident report to you before the end of the evening." He could hotspot his laptop to his cell phone outside Gwenyth's tent where he fully planned to park his Land Rover for the night.

"Shoot!" Tess mashed a button on the remote control, and the screen went black. "It's past closing time. Just get it to me before the weekend is over, alright?" She scooted off the edge of her desk and strode to the side of the room where her row of black metal filing cabinets were neatly lined up. She noisily opened and closed a few drawers, withdrew a couple of sheets of paper, and stuffed them in a cream file folder. "Here." She crossed the room to hand the folder to him. "You know how much I love computers. Do me a favor and write it out long-hand, will you?"

*Ugh!* Jett was pretty sure nobody but Tess hand-wrote anything out these days. He'd have to fish around for a pen before he left for the day. "Whatever makes you happy, boss." After keeping her truck most of the day and missing so many hours of work, he supposed he owed her one.

Tess snorted and returned to her desk to yank open another drawer. "Brad said you did a nice job out there on the cliff today." She unearthed another folder, licked her thumb, and riffled through a few papers. "The best job he's ever seen from any search and rescue operation, and that's worth something, coming from him. Brad's been working in forestry longer than me."

"That means a lot." Jett wasn't sure where this conversation was heading, but he was glad Tess wasn't ripping him a new backside over today's incident. "It felt good, too, being out there." He wasn't sure where the words came from, but he suddenly wanted Tess to know. To understand.

"I'm listening." She didn't look up from her paperwork, but a sly smile stole across her features.

He shook his head at her and plowed onward. "Helping someone like that. It felt good. It felt right."

She nodded. "Brad said you were a natural. That

you kept your head screwed on straight and kept the victim talking. He said you checked just about everything off the list in a proper textbook rescue op, right up to the point where you overrode his decision to call for an ambulance."

Jett clenched his jaw, still unable to explain that part of his actions even to his own satisfaction. "Yeah, I might have let my personal feelings get in the way there." That was as honest as he could be on the topic.

"Personal feelings, eh?" This time, Tess looked up, green eyes wide and glinting with interest. "Had you and Dr. Moore previously met?"

"No, ma'am."

"I'll be darn!" She tossed her papers down on the desk and rested her chin on her hands. "Well, out with it! I might be your supervisor, but I'm still a girl. Details! Details!"

"I don't know what happened. It's hard to put into words."

"Well, try!"

He chuckled and shook his head. "If you insist." He tried to choose his words carefully. "I want to be more than friends with her." Oh, this was painful! Why couldn't Tess just let it go, already?

Tess's gaze took on a dreamy cast. "Just invite me to the wedding."

"Tess!" he warned, feeling his face turn red.

"We've not even been on a date yet." Soon, though. He hoped it would be soon.

"And name your firstborn after your favorite boss."

He choked and had to cover it with a cough.

"Oh, Channing! You're so much fun to mess with," Tess chortled. She returned her attention to the papers she'd been fiddling with. "Back to business, though. One of our search and rescue guys has put in a transfer request to Dallas. His father isn't doing so well health-wise and needs looking after. Anyhow," she folded her hands atop her desk and pierced him with a searching gaze, "you're the first name that came to mind for his replacement, especially after today."

"Replacement!" He frowned at her. "I'm a forest ranger. I'm very good at being a forest ranger. It's not something I'm looking to give up."

"I'm not asking you to give up anything." She rolled her eyes and held out another stack of papers. "I'm asking you to consider adding something to your resume. Being on one of our search and rescue teams would involve a trip to Disaster City, where you'd spend a month training in various search and rescue techniques. What we specifically need more of here at the Sam Houston National Forest is tracking and scenting — both to help locate missing persons from time to time and work with local law enforcement to discourage and help prosecute poachers."

Jett stared at the papers in her hands. "Tracking and scenting sounds like K9 work."

"It is. Part of your training would entail becoming a certified dog handler." She waved the papers at him. "This is the application to become Jeff's replacement. I've also included a separate application to the Disaster City Search and Rescue Academy. Why don't you think about it a few days, and let me know?"

"I'll think about it," he accepted the applications, holding her gaze steadily, "but I already know my answer." He enjoyed his work as a forest ranger, but there were times it seemed a little tame compared to his past life on the championship power lifting circuit.

She gave him a satisfied smile, one that was edged with indulgent approval. "I can see that."

For about the ten thousandth time in the past two years, Jett was glad he'd come to work for Tess Wheeler. She'd turned out to be a great mentor and a solid soundboarder. She was steady, dependable, and — though they looked nothing alike — she reminded him of the mother he'd lost nearly seven years earlier.

"My answer is yes." He was pushing thirty and nearly panting with longing to sink his teeth into the next big challenge — something that would get his adrenaline pumping again. He missed that coveted rush of excitement, the feeling that what he was doing was meaningful and worthwhile, and the sense of accomplishment that always followed.

"Good." Tess's green eyes twinkled. "Now go check on that future wife of—"

He pressed his hands over his ears, papers and all, and spun in his boots to face the door. "I can't hear you. Bye!"

## CHAPTER 4: TEXTS AND TWEETS

GWENYTH

Gwenyth had always dreamed of being famous someday, but she'd been thinking more along the lines of writing a bestselling book about herbal remedies. That and signing autographed copies — not become notorious overnight, simply for being rescued off the side of a cliff by the hunky Jett Channing.

It was painful returning to work on Monday in a navy pinstriped suit and peep-toe heels, knowing nearly every set of eyes in the department was on her. She kept her head down, her briefcase clutched tightly in one hand, and her injured wrist cradled carefully in front of her. To her surprise, she made it down the long, tiled hallway without being stopped. The moment she stepped inside her sunlit, third-story office, however, she was waylaid by her geeky executive assistant, Echo Marcello.

"Please, please, *please*," she gushed, reaching for Gwenyth's right hand to cradle her cast gently between her hands, "assure me he signed your cast!"

Echo was a goth with a lab rat twist. She was impossibly tiny, but she made up for her lack of height by her outlandish and eclectic platform shoe and boot collection. She wore her long black hair straight with a perfect fringe of bangs across her pale forehead. Instead of solid black makeup, however, she deviated from the straight-up goth look by adding streaks of glittering blue or green beneath her dark eyeliner that always made Gwenyth think of electric sparks. Her clothing was usually dark and formfitting, but it almost always contained some sort of surprise. Today was no exception. Her sheer cardigan was woven from thousands of tiny silver threads in the shape of spiderwebs.

"No signature?" Echo crouched down in her silver stilettos to get a better look at the bottom of Gwenyth's cast. Her expressive mouth turned down at the corners. "I'm wildly disappointed."

"Look again." Gwenyth chuckled and flipped her wrist over. A skillful sketch of a panther was leaping across the underside of her stark white cast in black ink.

"Whoa! Let me see that again." Echo's expression perked up. "That is one killer panther. I'm still disappointed in you about the whole missed autograph opportunity," she waved her hands in an exaggerated circle, "but I am all *over* that panther ink. Who's the artist?" She click-clacked her way across the office to fill two fresh mugs of coffee and returned to sit one of them on Gwenyth's desk.

Accustomed to Echo's frequent dramatic outbursts, Gwenyth waited until Echo returned to her own desk before revealing the name of the artist. "Jett drew it."

Echo jolted so hard that Gwenyth inwardly congratulated herself on the timing of her statement. That was one hot coffee saved and probably an entire outfit in Echo's wardrobe, as well. "I'm in love," her assistant declared, pressing her hands to her heart and gazing up at the ceiling. "Lord have mercy! I've never even met the man, and I am totally in love with him, already." She gave a small bounce in her seat. "Oo, speaking of which...when do I get to meet him?" She gave a delicious shiver, picked up her mug to cradle it between her black lacquered fingertips, and shot Gwenyth a cheeky grin.

"I don't know," Gwenyth answered truthfully. "We just met." She gazed past their two desks to the wall of windows beyond. The morning sun was pouring inside the room, glinting off the microscopes and test tubes resting on the chrome cabinet that ran the length of the wall of windows.

"Oh, no. No, no, no!" Echo waved a finger in the air. "Don't even try to play the just-met game with me. I follow every viable news outlet in town from the newspaper to social media to you name it. Your crash introduction to Jett made it all the way to Twitter, I'll have you know!"

"Twitter?" Gwenyth squeaked. *Oh, say it isn't so!*

"You're on Twitter, honey!" Echo confirmed cheerfully. "And Instagram, Pinterest, Snapchat, and about a dozen other places. That's how I know that I know there is something going on between you and Jett Channing."

*I sure hope so!* Gwenyth's lips twitched at the memory of the way Jett had slept in his SUV outside her tent on Friday night, waking her every other hour with his low, husky baritone outside her tent walls to ensure she was alright. Then there was the exclusive dinner she'd shared with him last night on the rooftop of his penthouse. He'd sent a freaking limo to pick her up.

"See what I mean?" Echo waggled her brows, pointing. "That smile tells it all, Dr. Moore. You will *not* be keeping secrets from the world's most amazing executive assistant." The phone rang, forcing her to take a call.

Swallowing a longing sigh, Gwenyth set her briefcase down on the only clear spot atop her L-shaped desk and removed her laptop from it. Next she removed the precious little black plastic box she'd managed not to drop during her tumble over the side of the cliff. It still made her insides glow to think how Jett had refrigerated the rare flower overnight in her camping fridge and freezer combo unit to preserve it.

A vibration in her crossbody purse alerted her to a text message coming in on her cell phone. She had to set down the flower box to dig for her cell phone. *Ugh!* It was majorly inconvenient being a one-handed scientist.

She blinked at the screen and felt the heat rise to her cheeks. The message was from Jett.

*Just checking to make sure you survived the parade into work. — Jett*

The word "parade" said it all. Jett totally got how on display she'd felt ever since meeting him. He was no stranger to the paparazzi, himself, with years of experience under his belt; yet he still seemed to understand exactly how strange and difficult it was for her. That made it easier to deal with, somehow.

Hoping Echo didn't notice the heightened color in her cheeks, Gwenyth hastily wrote him back.

*I did. Thank you for asking. Hope your own entrance into work wasn't too tough. — Gwenyth*

He wrote back almost immediately. *Ha! I'm used to it. Trust me.*

"Oh. My. Gosh!" Echo's exclamation pulled Gwenyth from her rose-tinted reverie. "You're texting with him right now, aren't you?"

With a huff of sheer exasperation, Gwenyth set down her phone. "You do realize we're going to have to get back to work here, at some point?"

"Fine!" Sounding and looking a little miffed, Echo held up both hands. "Moving on. Moving on." Her expression twisted with doubt. "Well...*trying* to move on. Seriously, Gwenyth! You're going to have to be patient with me." She rolled her eyes and tipped her face to the ceiling. "This is the hardest thing anyone has ever asked of me. I mean," she lowered her voice to a hiss, "you're dating Jett Channing, for crying out loud! Jett Channing!" she added with a high-pitched squeal to her voice.

"That's it. I'm putting you in for a transfer." Gwenyth stood and moved to stand behind one of the microscopes at the counter.

"You wouldn't!" Echo gasped. "I'm a permanent fixture here."

*Of course I wouldn't.* Gwenyth hid a smile. Her work at the university would seem frightfully dull without Echo's colorful, albeit sometimes distracting, brand of support. "I need one of those dual concavity slides. Do you have any idea where I stored the last batch?"

"Indeed I do, Dr. Moore, ma'am. I can take a hint. Yes, I can. Back to work, lackey." Still sounding anxious, she dug in a drawer, gloved up, and delivered one smudge-free concavity slide.

Gwenyth raised her brows as she accepted the slide, ever amazed at Echo's attention to detail despite her flighty personality. There couldn't have been so much as a speck of dust on the slide. Talk about no contamination!

"What?" Echo gave a distressed gasp. "What did I do wrong?"

"Nothing at all. You're amazing, and you know it. Might have to hold off on that transfer, after all."

Echo let out a gusty sigh of relief and placed one gloved hand over her heart. "You had me going there for a sec."

"No, I didn't." Gwenyth knew better than to fall for such a thinly veiled trick. "You were just trying to guilt me into revealing more about my personal life."

"Why, Dr. Moore!" Echo tried and failed to muffle a snicker. "I had no idea you possessed such a suspicious nature. I'm wounded. Truly wounded."

"Uh-huh." Gwenyth placed a sample of one of the most common coneflower petals on one side of the slide. Then she placed a sample of the rare breed of coneflower on the other side. She hydrated both samples with a single drop of distilled water and added a much smaller spec of blue dye. Next, she bent over the lens to adjust the magnification. "The limo he sent for me last night was black. Our dinner on the rooftop of his penthouse involved candles, roses, and—"

Echo gave a muffled shriek of rage. "I get it. I totally get it. I'll bug off. Promise!" She whipped off her rubber gloves, tossed them in the wastebasket, and click-clacked her way back to her desk. "There's no need to play me like that. If you want to keep secrets, well...I don't have to like it, but I'll respect it. Er...*try* to respect it," she amended.

"What?" Gwenyth raised her head in surprise to meet Echo's gaze. "You don't believe me?"

"Oh! You weren't kidding?" Echo's dark eyes grew round. "A black limousine, huh? Followed by candles and roses?"

Gwenyth nodded, smiling in awe. "It really happened. I'm still absorbing."

Echo dropped her elbows atop her desk and her head into her hands. "*You're* still absorbing. What about me?"

Gwenyth returned her attention to the vivid purple petals beneath her microscope. If her theory was correct, it was a rare breed of *Echinacea purpurea*, otherwise known as purple coneflower. She'd been studying the medicinal qualities of this particular flower for years, because of its anti-inflammatory, antioxidant, and anti-viral properties. She'd even written her doctoral dissertation on the topic.

As far as she was concerned, the petals of the *Echinacea* plant were living, blooming little miracles. Ever since her childhood bout with cancer, she'd been consuming or applying every viable commercial product on the market that contained *Echinacea* — from teas to liquid tinctures to capsules to tablets to ointments and lotions — all for its immune-strengthening benefits. And here she was at the age of twenty-six, cancer-free despite the eighty percent statistical likelihood that her tumor would have and should have returned by now.

"What is it?" Echo's voice was hushed. "I've seen that look before. It's your I-may-have-just-made-a-crazy-wonderful discovery look. Tell me what it is, so I can have the powers-that-be nominate you for a Pulitzer."

"I'm not sure, but crazy and wonderful probably aren't too far off the mark, if my theory is correct." Gwenyth raised her head from the microscope. "Want to come take a look?"

"I thought you'd never ask!" Rubbing her hands together in glee, Echo tiptoed her way across the room. "Just tell me what I'm looking for."

"Antioxidants. You know what they do, right?"

"Yep. They prevent the damage to our body's cells caused by free radicals. Trust me, doctor, I know all about taking antioxidant supplements. You don't get a bod like mine without lots of TLC and maintenance."

Gwenyth chuckled. That was probably the absolute best thing about working with Echo. The petite sprite of a woman always had a way of making Gwenyth laugh, even when they weren't discussing things that would normally be considered humorous. "I so love talking geek with you! Just for conversation's sake, what sort of free radicals might you be combatting at this time, love?"

"Huh!" Echo waved a hand. "Don't even get me started."

"Too late."

"Well, there's stress, unhealthy toxins and chemicals in the air, radiation from the sun..." She sighed dramatically. "All those pesky little things that strive to age us before our time, which I absolutely refuse to let happen to me, because..." she shot a secretive smile in Gwenyth's direction, "I've decided I'm going to live to be as old as Methuselah. I have so much I want to accomplish, and there's just no way I'll be able to get it all done in one lifetime."

"Alright, then, my dear immortal assistant." Living for hundreds of years was not something Gwenyth had ever aspired to do. She was still rejoicing over the fact she'd managed to reach the age of twenty-six. Then again, if her theory was correct about the rare breed of coneflower, who was she to say that extending life expectancy might not be in the realm of possibilities? "If you would direct your attention next to the tiny dots I've highlighted with blue dye and magnified many thousands of times over."

"They sure are pretty! What are they?" Echo demanded.

"Antioxidant agents," Gwenyth declared in excitement. "Now it's your turn. Tell me what you see. What's different between the two samples?"

Echo shrugged her delicate shoulders, "Well,

that's sort of obvious. The one on the left has a decent number of the antioxidant cells, but the one on the right appears to have bazillions more."

"Exactly!" Gwenyth snapped her fingers. "I'm estimating at least three times as many, but it may be more than that. It'll require more testing to be sure this isn't a onetime anomaly." An aberration like a birth defect, for instance, causing a cluster of cells to become infused in only one region of the plant. She doubted that was the case, but for her findings to be taken seriously in the scientific community, she would need to prove it. It was going to take time, too. Since the breed of flower she'd discovered was so rare, she was going to have to grow her own from snippets taken from this very plant.

Gwenyth picked up the little miracle plant and twirled with it in the center of the room. "I'm going to call you Plant Zero, since you started it all."

"And you call *me* the geek around here," Echo sighed. "Next time you try to point fingers, I'll just have to remind you how you nerded-out and started talking to a plant. I'm pretty sure there's professional help for stuff like that."

"Ha! If my theory is correct, this little plant will be the professional help tens of thousands of people seek."

"You don't need to convince me." Echo whirled to face her, wearing a rapt expression on her face. "Just for the record, I believe you and fully endorse your theory here and now — many years ahead of all the FDA-required approvals and red tape. Feel free to have me taste-test and otherwise be your guinea pig for any and all future experiments." She smoothed a hand over her sleek black hair. "It's the most logical next step in my Echo-is-going-to-live forever campaign."

Grinning, Gwenyth happily spent the rest of the morning splicing sample offshoots from Plant Zero to soak in herbal water, so they could grow roots and germinate into new plants. She also carefully grafted two of the rare offshoots into regular coneflower plants to grow hybrids that could additionally be tested for their viability. Every so often, her work was interrupted by the telltale buzzing of her cell phone to indicate another text was coming in.

*Just checking on my favorite one-handed scientist. Doing alright? Still not overly thrilled you went into work with a concussion this morning. — Jett*

Sheesh! He sounded pretty possessive for a guy who had known her all of a few days, but Gwenyth was having trouble working up a single ounce of irritation over it. He was sweetly possessive in a romantic, non-suffocating sort of way. She'd missed having a special someone in her life who cared. If she was being entirely honest with herself, she and John had been growing apart for a long time. The real breakup, at least the emotional severance part of it, had happened a good three or four months ago, making her suspect that Yasmin had been in John's life much longer than he claimed.

Nibbling on her lower lip, Gwenyth tried a new tactic on her next text message. Maybe Jett wasn't a scientist like John, but that didn't mean he couldn't appreciate her big discovery in his own way.

*I made a big discovery this morning.*

*So did I,* he shot back. *I can't stop thinking about you.*

She crouched down behind her computer screen, blushing and praying Echo wouldn't notice.

*Am I scaring you?* He wrote again before she could think of an appropriate response.

*No.* She pushed send. Then a comeback came to her, and she started typing again. *I'm a scientist armed with test tubes and deadly chemicals. I don't scare easily.*

He sent back a laughing emoji. *Uh-oh. Sounds like I should be the one who's scared.*

*Are you?* She enjoyed taunting him.

*Not even a little, beautiful.*

In seconds, he was typing again. *Got to run an errand into the city in about an hour. Want to catch lunch with me?*

*It depends,* she teased. *Where will you take me?*

He sent a meme of a white SUV zooming across her screen. A caption followed. *Anywhere you want, so long as we can get there quickly. — A very lonely, very hungry forest ranger*

*Then I'll have to say...* She pushed send and waited.

*So cruel!* He sent her a picture of a rose with thorns.

*Yes,* she typed, leaving it open to interpretation as to whether she was agreeing to go to lunch with him or simply agreeing she was cruel.

*I can be there by* 1:30.

*And If I'm not ready that soon?* She sent him a meme of a mad scientist exploding test tubes in his lab.

*No worries. I'll just stand beneath your office window and serenade you until you're ready.* He sent her a meme of a Mexican quartet in large sombreros, playing accordions and maracas.

*Can you sing?*

*Care to find out?* His response made her laugh out loud.

Gwenyth clapped a hand over her mouth.

"That's okay. Go ahead and keep sharing super secret texts with your man, Jett. I'm good with it. A-okay." Echo lifted her chin as if bracing herself. "I've got my promise of a lifelong supply of antioxidants from you to remove all the stress you're causing me right now by leaving me in the dark."

Gwenyth snickered. "He's taking me to lunch, alright?"

"Is that all?" Echo gave a mock huff. "You've been texting for over ten minutes."

"But who's counting?" Gwenyth teased.

"Have a little pity, will you?" Echo retorted. "I'm in a dry spell over here."

"Really?" Gwenyth frowned. "I thought you were dating one of our medical students."

"That's what I thought, but we haven't been on a date in four whole nights. First, he was on call. Then he claimed he had a big evaluation to prepare for."

"Sounds about right, considering he's in med school," Gwenyth mused, wondering what was the problem.

"Who's side are you on?" Echo demanded. "Listen, lady, I'm not looking for the voice of reason. I'm looking for sympathy." She wrinkled her nose. "Or a blind date if Jett Channing has any single, hot body-builder friends."

Gwenyth chuckled. "You're a complete nut!"

Echo made a pouty face. "A very lonely, neglected one."

GWENYTH WAS grateful there were no rolling cameras or reporters holding boom mikes when she stepped onto the sidewalk outside her office building. Nowadays, she never knew when one might step into her path without warning. Come to think of it, they could be hiding, though, like a sniper...just waiting for her to step into the crosshairs of their camera lens.

She glanced furtively around the university grounds and parking lot but saw nothing amiss.

A white Land Rover zoomed into the parking lot and cruised up to where she was standing. The tinted window lowered, and Jett's handsome face appeared. "Looking for a ride, beautiful?"

## CHAPTER 5: NEXT STEPS

### JETT

Jett's pulse accelerated at the sight of Gwenyth in her work clothes. He'd dated plenty of beautiful women before, but she was different. Stunning, in fact. The kind of stunning that took his breath away and made his thoughts bumble dizzily around his head and run right smack into one other.

Normally he cracked his window and instructed his dates to leap inside the vehicle. That way both of them could hunker down from the paparazzi behind his specially tinted windows as soon as possible, but he didn't feel like rushing Gwenyth that way. Instead, he was the one who did the leaping, hurrying around the SUV to open the door for her.

Out of habit, though, he kept his head down. "Professor." He ushered her inside, taking great pleasure in the sight of her killer heels and the way her creamy slender legs looked in them.

To his crazy delight, she twisted in his direction and placed her one good hand for leverage on his shoulder as she mounted the running board. "Are we back to titles, then, Mr. Channing?" Her glorious red hair was piled atop her head in some sort of complicated twist, but a few touchable wisps had pulled loose and were tumbling around her temples and cheeks.

"Aw, come on!" he teased, leaning across her to buckle her seatbelt. He told himself it was to speed things up, since she was sporting a cast; but the truth was, he just wanted an excuse to be close to her. "Every guy with red blood running through his veins has a fantasy that involves a gorgeous professor in dark-rimmed glasses."

"Every guy, huh?" She tipped her face down to stare over the rims of her spectacles, so he could get the full effect of her eye roll.

"This one sure does."

She blushed so hotly that his breathing felt off when he firmly shut the passenger door.

"So did the ravenous ranger decide on lunch?" Her voice was light and teasing as he took his seat behind the wheel.

"He did." Jett shot her a sideways glance and winked, wondering what she would say next.

"Is it a state secret?"

"Maybe."

"Fine." She raised her chin. "Then I'll just have

to bore you with the full report of my major scientific discovery while you drive."

"I'm intrigued." He couldn't recall being more intrigued about anything else in a very long time. Maybe whatever she was about to say would shed more light on the mystery behind the girl he was fast falling for.

"Sure you are."

"Try me," he shot back as he sped down the freeway.

"It involves antioxidants and free radicals," she warned in a mock threatening voice.

"I take it, this has something to do with that blasted flower you risked life and limb to harvest?" He arched his brows at her.

Her smile widened. "Very good, Mr. Channing. If this was a test, that deduction would have earned you some solid points."

"Thank you." Without thinking, he reached across the cab to take her hand.

She caught her breath and lapsed into silence. Unless he was mistaken, her fingers trembled slightly in his.

"You okay over there?" He was inwardly kicking himself for holding her hand. It was too soon.

"We're going so fast."

He knew she wasn't referring to the speed of his vehicle. "I know."

"Doesn't it scare you?" She sounded uncertain.

He hardly knew how to answer her. "Maybe if it didn't feel so right."

She caught her breath again.

He turned his Land Rover into a city park. A group of women in shorts and ponytails were clustered near the front entrance, chatting and holding beverages, while a bevy of children scampered around the playground. He drove past the playground equipment and gazebos, past picnic benches and a lake, until they reached a gravel drive with a security gate. He had to park and get out to punch in the code to open the gate.

To his relief, a quizzical smile was playing around Gwenyth's lips when he slid back in the SUV and met her gaze.

"This definitely is *not* what I was expecting in the way of a lunch venue."

"Good. I wanted to surprise you." He drove until they came to a spring that gushed and bubbled its way down a rocky wall into a creek.

"Oh, wow!" she breathed, staring raptly at the water feature. "It's lovely."

"Yes." He resisted the urge to lean over and sample all that awe and joy on her lips.

Her lashes fluttered against her cheeks.

"I brought along a picnic lunch." He opened his door, grabbed the basket and blanket from the back, and walked around to the passenger door to assist her down.

She balanced on her tiptoes in the pea gravel, making Jett realize he'd made one grave mistake. Girls in heels can't walk in gravel. It probably wasn't too easy for them to walk in sod, either. In the end, Gwenyth solved the problem for them by stepping out of her shoes and setting them on the floorboard of his truck. She walked barefoot at his side, which allowed him to admire her siren orange lacquered toenails.

He set out the quilt and picnic basket at the base of the falls, just far enough away to miss the over-spray. Then he motioned for Gwenyth to take a seat.

She settled on the blanket with a sigh and shaded her eyes to take in their surroundings. "If you don't mind me asking, where are we?"

"It's a weekend getaway that a buddy of mine owns. There's a cabin over the next hill."

He didn't miss the twinge of a grimace before her face cleared.

"Before you ask, no," he stated firmly. "I've never brought another woman here. You're the first."

She turned her startled blue gaze to his. "I wasn't going to ask that."

"You were thinking it."

She chuckled knowingly but didn't deliver a comeback.

He lowered himself to the blanket and laid all the way back, propping an arm across his forehead to shade his eyes.

"I thought you said you were a very hungry ranger," she teased.

He squinted up at her. "I also said I was a very lonely one, and now I'm not." He reached for her hand again. He wasn't very hungry any longer, either. "Can we talk about this? About us?"

She nodded slowly, looking painfully shy and jumpy. "Okay."

"I know we've only been dating a few days, and I know we both just went through very public breakups."

She bit her lower lip and nodded again.

"If I had any sense whatsoever, I would have never allowed this to happen so soon."

She paled and averted her face, but he tightened his fingers on hers. "What I'm trying to say is, I don't want to be your rebound, and I sure as heck don't want you to be my rebound. I want more than that. I want you to be mine, Gwenyth Moore. No strings attached to past relationships. Just mine."

To his horror, mist dimmed the sparkle in her eyes.

"Please don't cry," he pleaded softly. "I wasn't trying to make you cry."

"That's the trouble with rebounds." Her voice shook as she swiveled her face to his at last. "We're both still so..." she blinked a few times and swallowed hard, "so muckied up in the head, emotionally speaking."

"I know." He rubbed his thumb in circles across the top of her hand, hoping to soothe her. "But please understand I didn't plan on meeting you. I didn't plan on falling beneath your spell so quickly or so completely. I didn't plan on thinking about you every minute of every day since the moment I carried you across that guard rail. It just happened, and I feel powerless to stop it."

She closed her eyes and tipped her head back to allow the sun to spill across her more fully. "I think about you, too, Jett. Way more than I should."

His heart sang at her admission. That's all he needed to hear. The rest of the things he wanted to say could wait. "Hey." He rolled to his side to face her. "You never finished telling me about your big discovery."

Her shoulders relaxed at the change in conversation. She opened her eyes, a soft smile playing around her lips.

"You sure you want me to go in full science mode on you?"

"We-e-e-ll...since you asked, feel free to give me the Science for Dummies version." He flipped open the lid of the picnic basket. "You're, by far, the smartest woman I've ever eaten lunch with, but I'll try to keep up."

She laughed. "As a bodybuilder, I'm sure you're well aware of the health benefits of antioxidants."

"I am." He was relieved that he understood her

thus far. "They're in everything. Some health nuts consider them the holy grail of supplements and shovel down every version they can get their hands on. Teas, capsules, you name it. You'd think they'd discovered the fountain of youth."

Gwenyth shook her head, a merry twinkle in her eyes. "You sound like my executive assistant. She just this morning swore to be my guinea pig and chief taste-tester, since one of her biggest goals is to live forever."

"I like her already." Jett pulled two wrapped packages out of the picnic basket and set one in Gwenyth's lap.

"Everybody likes Echo. She's one of those people who are impossible not to like." Gwenyth grinned, just thinking about the artful and amusing ways Echo was going to ply Gwenyth with questions about her lunch date when she returned to the office. "Anyhow, the flower I found is a rare form of the *Echinacea* species."

He arched a brow at her. "The American coneflower?"

"*Echinacea purpurea*, to be exact. The rarest form of it."

"I am very happy to say that I'm keeping up with you so far. Go on." He peeled his lobster salad wrap from the paper and took a bite. It was drenched in a top-secret house dressing from the most exclusive caterer in town. He hoped Gwenyth liked it.

"The first test I ran it through this morning showed it was infused with at least three times as many antioxidants as a regular coneflower petal."

"That's huge, babe!" His delighted gaze met her surprised one. That was when he realized what he'd called her. He sat up the rest of the way. "When the time comes, I'll be standing right beside Echo in line for taste-testing." He paused a beat. "And endorsements."

She recoiled in horror. "Oh, Jett! I didn't tell you all this because I was trying to wheedle a favor—"

"Oh course you didn't!" He was dismayed that his attempt at showing his support had been so misinterpreted. "Sheesh, Gwenyth!" He shook his head at her. "I'm just trying to be supportive here. I can't help that my support might come with a few extra perks." It was something she was simply going to have to get used to.

"I, ah...okay." She wrinkled her brow at him. "Just so long as you don't think I was trying to...er..."

"I don't." He angled his head at the package in her lap. "Are you ready for lunch?"

It was so awkward for her to unwrap her sandwich with one hand that he ended up doing it for her. And holding it to her lips so she could take her first bite...

"It's good." She nodded at him. "Very good!"

He waited until she'd taken a few more bites

before he moved on with his next bit of news. "I have something big to tell you, too."

"Really?" She looked genuinely curious, another thing he adored about her. She was just so...in-the-moment and real.

"There's a vacancy on one of our search and rescue teams at the national forest. I applied for the job this morning."

"Well, congratulations!" She looked a little puzzled. "Does this mean you won't be a forest ranger any longer?"

"Not at all. I'll be a forest ranger and a certified K9 handler for tracking and scenting."

Her expression lit. "You'll get to work with dogs!"

"Let me guess. You love dogs," he teased.

"I've wanted one for as long as I can remember," she confessed, "but, growing up, I always lived in apartments. And now I live in a condo without a private yard." She shook her head. "Someday, I'm going to get a dog or two or three, when I finally have a place for them to run."

"I can definitely see a few dogs in your future." *In our future.* He blinked to erase the thought. *Too soon to be thinking in plurals.* "If I get the job, my supervisor will be sending me to the Disaster City Search and Rescue Academy for a month of training."

"How soon will you find out about the job?"

"I'm their top choice, and it sounds like the DCSRA has an opening for me in their April program. Plus, there's some forestry conference they want me to attend later this week and a K9 training course after that to get me ready for the academy."

"That's a pretty hectic travel schedule." She lowered her sandwich to her lap.

"Yes, but it's temporary."

"Where exactly is the academy located?"

"About a three-hour drive from here." He waved a hand. "Up near Dallas."

"A little far for a lunch date." There was a hint of a sigh in her voice that tugged at his heart and gave him hope.

"Not on the weekends." He reached for her sandwich and set it back in the picnic basket. Then he scooted closer to toy with her fingers. "I wouldn't be allowed to leave. I checked, but you would be allowed to visit." He ducked his head, unable to meet her inscrutable expression. "If you want. No pressure. Or you could use that time to put on the brakes and slow down...whatever this is... happening between us."

"Is that what you want?" Her voice was barely above a whisper, "to put on the brakes?"

His head came up, shocked that she felt the need to ask. "No," he assured softly. "I should," he amended hastily, "everything considered. I should give you your space. Breakups are brutal. I should give you time to mend and heal, but no. That's not what I want."

"Maybe I'll visit, then."

He held her gaze, drinking in her shy admiration, reveling in her hesitant capitulation. "I'd like that. A lot." He reached up to touch her cheek. "There is something else I'd like." His gaze dropped to her lush lips that still boasted a tinge of gloss, despite the lunch they'd eaten.

"What?" she whispered.

The air between them fairly sparked with the intensity of their awareness of each other.

"For you to send me off with a kiss." He tenderly brushed back one of the fiery tendrils of hair a light breeze was making dance against her cheek. "More than anything, that's what I'd like to take with me."

They swayed closer to each other. In the end, Jett wasn't certain if it was his hopeless longing for her kiss that drew her like a magnet, or if she was the one who closed the final distance between them. All he knew was their lips touched. And it was perfect. Like tasting sunshine. Or heaven.

She was all soft, trembly, and sweet. He cupped the curve of her neck but felt her go still when he tried to deepen the kiss.

He immediately raised his head, worried that he'd done something wrong. "Is everything alright, babe? With us, I mean?"

She made a gasping sound. "It will be."

"Okay, now you have me worried."

"Jett!" His name came out as a breathy expulsion. "You just turned my whole world upside down."

He tipped his forehead against hers. "In a good way or a bad way?"

Her laugh was shaky. "It's so much so soon. I'm happy. I'm terrified. I don't even know what to say next."

"I do." Relief surged through him so strongly that it made him giddy. "This feeling." He took her hand and drew back far enough to gaze deeply into her eyes. "If you and I are meant to be, it'll still be here when I get back." He laced his fingers through hers.

"I think I'm going to miss you," she confessed, cheeks turning rosy.

"I *know* I'm going to miss you, babe." He shook his head at her. "I already do." A month suddenly felt like a very long time. However, it was a month she needed. A month they both needed, if they were going to make this work.

"So this is goodbye." There was a wistful hitch in her voice.

"For now." He stood and tugged her to her feet. "But I'll be back. That's a promise."

## CHAPTER 6: NEW PARTNER

### JETT

Jett left town the next day. He could still feel the imprint of Gwenyth's lips on his the entire flight to Seattle. And the farther he flew, the more fearful he became. At almost thirty years of age, he'd been around long enough to recognize something truly rare and valuable when it crossed his path. Or in this case, someone.

He'd met champion athletes and celebrities from all over the world. He'd been introduced to diplomats, heads of state, and even royalty. He knew what it was like to feel the shock and awe of shaking the hand of a foreign ambassador or other dignitary. But none of those feelings compared to what it felt like to meet Dr. Gwenyth Moore for the first time.

A petite and dusty red-headed minx of a research scientist who had foolishly risked, well...*everything* to chase down a single flower in the hopes of improving the plight of mankind. She'd broken her wrist and her glasses in the process, and Lord only knew how many minutes she'd been from losing her grip on that flimsy vine and tumbling the rest of the way over the cliff. She wasn't just a desk warmer or a paycheck collector. She truly believed that what she did mattered, that her research could make a difference.

And she wasn't motivated by any of the usual suspects, things like fame or fortune. In fact, she'd balked pretty loudly at even the mention of receiving an endorsement from him, like she considered it to be cutting a corner. Or cheating, somehow.

Nope. Dr. Gwenyth Moore was the real thing — from her riot of red hair all the way down to the four-inch heels she wore to boost her less-than-average height.

Jett rode down a swell of air turbulence that matched the turbulence in his soul. It was emotionally staggering to him to contemplate just how many ways his and Gwenyth's paths could have failed to cross.

What if Gwenyth had never become ill with her tumor? Her parents might have never relocated their family from New Zealand. Or what if they'd chosen to pursue medical care for her in some other country besides the United States? Then there was the possibility Jett least wanted to consider: What if Gwenyth hadn't survived her fight with cancer? That was the biggest what-if. He'd done a little research of his own about childhood cancer in the past few days. According to the information he'd found, Gwenyth was defying all stats to be in remission for this long. Did it have something to do with her research on antioxidants? Was she self-testing her theories? There was so much he didn't yet know about her, but he wanted to. In fact, he wanted to know everything there was to know about this amazing woman.

What he did know was...she'd survived her battle with cancer, and her family had subsequently settled in Pasadena. What were the odds twenty-something years later that she would accept a position as a research scientist in the very town he lived in? He supposed the odds were even slimmer that she'd chosen to go camping at the national forest he worked at, and gotten herself injured in the process of chasing down a flower. And that their regular search and rescue teams had already been deployed to handle other emergencies, so he'd been pulled in to rescue the very woman who would capture his heart...

When Jett traced the likelihood of all the circumstances falling into place in order for him to meet Gwenyth, he could come up with one answer only. It was a miracle. Not just luck or happenstance, but a God-thing. Something that was meant to be.

It was awe-inspiring and overwhelming, breathtaking and humbling. He bowed his head right there on the airplane, overcome with the enormity of the gift he'd been given. "Thank you, Lord," he whispered. He didn't know how long he would have Gwenyth in his life. He didn't know if the cancer would return or if some other calamity would befall one of them. All he knew was he would cherish every day they had together.

But first, there was the forestry conference in Seattle, then a specialized K9 handler course in Melody, Wyoming, followed by the Disaster City Search and Rescue Academy training near Dallas. The forestry conference turned out to be a bit on the ho-hum side. Jett was glad when it was over.

The dog handler training, however, was excellent. His instructor was a tall, firm-jawed blonde deputy named Amber Snow with more than a decade in law enforcement and over twenty years of experience in training dogs. She made Jett think of a younger version of Tess Wheeler. After their class of eight men and two women received several live K9 demonstrations on scenting and tracking, they broke into smaller groups to begin the process of training one-on-one with the dogs.

He soon discovered that all his other classmates had traveled to Melody with their own dogs. He stayed after class on the second day of the week-long course to consult with Deputy Snow.

"Ma'am. I know we're already two days into the course, but I'd like to finish my training with a dog of my own. Problem is, I'm not from this area and don't know any of the local breeders. Can you point me in the right direction?"

She shrugged. "It depends. How serious you are about dog handling, Channing? We always recommend you bring your own dog to get the maximum results from this course. Just curious. Did you miss that memo?"

He made a face. "I'm going with option A. Yes, I missed the memo. The job opportunity and this trip came on kind of suddenly, but that doesn't mean I'm not serious about dog handling. More importantly, I'm very serious about saving lives. That's what brought me here. So if you help me acquire a dog, I promise I'll put in whatever extra hours it'll require to catch him up on the training we've already covered."

"Well, how can I say no to that?" Deputy Snow's tough stance relaxed. "Follow me, Channing. I have someone I'd like you to meet."

He followed her out of the main classroom and into the kennel next door. They were immediately greeted with a cacophony of yips and barks as the dogs in cages clamored for attention, hopeful they were about to be released for a run. Jett hated seeing so many dogs in cages. He knew it was only a temporary boarding situation, but still...

The deputy escorted him down the long hallway of cages to the one at the very end. Inside was a glossy, full-grown golden retriever with his head resting on his paws.

"Hey, buddy." Jett squatted down in front of the cage and was instantly drawn to the sadness in the dog's eyes. Grief was something he recognized. It looked the same on just about every creature. He was willing to bet this dog had suffered a recent loss.

"This is Major." Amber Snow's voice was hushed and reverent. "He's four-years-old and already trained in scenting and tracking. In fact, this dog has seen more action than a lot of cops I know."

"What's his story?" Jett braced himself.

She was silent a moment. "You might've seen it on the news. He belonged to the sheriff who dove in the lake after that school bus."

"Yeah. I did." Jett scrubbed a hand over his face. It was a tragedy that had taken place only a week ago. "Man! I'm sorry, Major." He remembered the story all too well. The sheriff had helped get the few children on board to safety, then had gone back after the driver who'd suffered a heart attack. Unfortunately, the bus had rolled and pinned him beneath it. Both men had perished.

Deputy Snow shook her head. "Though not specifically trained in water rescues, Major dragged a small kid to safety, then went back in — we suspect — after his handler. He swam in circles around the site of the sinking bus and barked until he was hoarse. The first responders weren't certain they would ever get him to come out of the water."

"Wow!" Jett's voice cracked. He had to clear his throat before speaking again. "Major sounds exactly like the kind of partner I'd like to have by my side." He scrubbed his hand over his face again and faced the dog. "What do you say, buddy? Would you like to honor your sheriff's name by getting back out there and making a difference again?"

As if sensing the tremendous empathy and respect Jett was feeling, the golden retriever thumped his tail a few times on the ground.

Jett stood and reached for the latch on the cage. "Mind if he and I spend some time getting to know each other?"

"Knock yourself out, Channing." Deputy Snow nodded in satisfaction. "The rest of the evening is yours to spend however you wish. Just remember search and rescue dogs aren't lap dogs." She angled her head at the collection of padded uniforms hanging against the wall opposite the dog cages. "Might want to wear the bite pads for your first pow-wow."

"Thank you, Deputy Snow." Jett waited until she left the kennel before squatting down beside the cage again. "Here's the deal, Major. I'm on a time crunch, so I'd kinda like to skip the part about the bite pads, if you're willing."

Major thumped his tail again.

"I'm going to just let myself inside your cage and have a man-to-man about a few things. Think you can handle that, old boy?"

Major blinked and watched Jett as he slowly stood and reached for the latch to the gate. Without dropping the dog's gaze, he stepped inside the cage, shut it behind him, and stood there in silence for several minutes.

Initially, the dog growled low in his throat at the invasion into his space, but his head never came off his paws.

Jett lowered himself at a sloth-like pace to sit beside the creature. He stretched his long legs out in front of him, facing the dog. Major's eyes rolled upward to inspect the newcomer, and another low growl rumbled in the back of his throat.

"I hear you, old boy." Jett unwaveringly held the dog's sad gaze, exerting himself as the alpha in the small, enclosed space. "I'm not the fellow you were hoping would come walking through that gate. I don't look, smell, or sound familiar, but that doesn't change one big undeniable fact. We need each other." He kept a steady dialogue going in a low, soothing voice to give the dog time to grow accustomed to his sound and scent.

"I got a girl for you to help me protect back home, old boy. Her name is Dr. Gwenyth Moore, and you're going to fall in love with her the moment you meet her." *Just like I did.*

Jett's breathing grew rough as he finally acknowledged the thing that had been nagging the back of his mind for days. He wasn't just crushing on Gwenyth. He wasn't just fantasizing about the latest beauty he was dating. He was truly and honestly missing the woman he loved. A woman who was brilliant and kindhearted, vibrant and full of life...unlike the brave sheriff poor Major was grieving his canine heart out for.

"I'm sorry you lost a partner, Major, but at least he died a hero. That's a risk I'll be asking you to take all over again if you agree to our new partnership. You could lose me, or I could lose you, but it's a risk worth taking. A risk that could save many more lives if we team up and work together."

The dog stared him down for more than an hour, just blinking and listening. After a while, Jett needed to use the restroom, but he knew he couldn't afford to take a break — not yet. Not until Major yielded and accepted him as his new master. It was a crucial point on which Jett couldn't afford to compromise. It would set the tone for their entire relationship going forward. Or so the trainers had claimed during his first two days of classes... Jett had zero background working with dogs, so he had no choice but to believe what he'd been taught.

Dinner time rolled around for the residents in the kennel. There was much rejoicing as the tech on duty made her rounds to fill the dogs' food bowls and freshen up their water. Jett listened with interest as the young woman instructed each dog to go stand by their food bowl before entering the cage. The command was two simple words: *Food bowl!*

Major's ears perked each time the tech gave the command to the next dog in line, but he never looked her way. He continued to watch Jett.

"You're hungry, aren't you, old boy?" Jett asked softly.

Major made a whining sound but still didn't raise his head.

"He's hardly eaten three bites since he lost the sheriff." The tech paused outside Major's cage with a sigh. "It's been a week. If someone doesn't get him to eat soon..." She sighed again. "Food bowl, Major."

He twitched his ears but otherwise ignored the tech. He was still too busy staring Jett down.

Jett put on his most ferocious frown and infused a bit of bite into his tone. "Food bowl, Major!" He leaned forward menacingly while he gave the command.

With a squeal that sounded dangerously close to a sob, the creature dragged himself to his feet, as if the movements were exhausting, and loped across the cage to stand in front of his bowl.

Jett tipped his head back against the cage in relief. He'd won the staring match. This was progress — real progress — the kind of progress that had to take place before he and Major could start training together.

"Well, I'll be darn!" the tech breathed. She opened the latch to the cage and started to step inside.

"I'll feed him." Jett reached for the bucket of food. "From now on, I'll handle his food and water. Me and no one else, okay?"

"No problem." She handed over the pail of dog food. "I'm just glad he finally decided to eat. No one else has been able to get through to him, though not for lack of trying." She arched her set of well-manicured black brows at him. "Who are you? The dog whisperer?" Humor infused her voice.

"His new partner, actually. Jett Channing."

The young woman didn't so much as flicker an eyelash. Jett held back a chuckle, knowing it probably meant she had no idea who he was. The puppies and kittens silkscreened on her scrubs indicated she was more likely an avid watcher of Animal Planet than any sports channel. That was fine with him. He didn't get to enjoy anonymity very often and treasured each time someone treated him like a regular guy.

She nodded and stepped back from Major's cage. "Feeding times are 9:00 a.m. and 6:00 p.m. Food is in the unlocked closet at the front of the kennel, along with the dog biscuits. We don't issue treats around here for looking cute, only as a reward for good behavior when the dogs follow our commands."

"Roger that." Jett offered her a mock salute and proceeded to feed Major. "I'll be back in a bit, buddy. Gotta use the facilities."

Major raised his head from his food dish to watch Jett as he left the cage.

Jett turned around to face him. "Eat, Major!"

The dog lowered his head and returned to his dinner.

"Seriously. That's pretty amazing." The tech followed Jett towards the door. "I'm Laura, by the way."

"Nice to meet you, Laura." She had a fresh-faced country girl look and was probably half his age.

She trotted to keep up with his long stride while he traveled the parking lot and headed for the resident cabins. "You were really good with Major back there. How long have you been training dogs?"

Jett spared her a sideways glance. "This is my first time, so I'll take that as a compliment."

"You're kidding!" She halted in her tracks when he mounted the porch to the cabin he was sharing with three other classmates.

"I wish I was." He paused with his hand on the door knob, well aware he had a long way to go before achieving the status of a proficient dog handler. "It was nice meeting you, Laura."

"Same here, sir. Enjoy the rest of your evening."

*Sir? Ouch!* Jett grinned at the term of respect, knowing it fully planted him in the category of *old man* in the eyes of the teen. He let himself in the cabin and quickly took care of his human needs — showering, grabbing a quick bite to eat, and brushing his teeth. The cabin reminded him of his old college dorm with two bedrooms on each side that shared a bathroom and a common area in the middle that consisted of a kitchenette with a bistro table and stools, living room, and laundry closet.

Snagging a bottle of water from the drink fridge, Jett headed outside. He dialed Gwenyth as he made his way back to the kennel.

She picked up on the second ring. "Hello?"

"Hey, you." It was amazing just hearing her voice. Getting to speak with her a few minutes each evening was seriously the highlight of his day. "How are those coneflower experiments going?"

"Well...I think I can safely say that Echo is one step closer to living forever." He could hear the smile in her voice.

"Making the world a better place, one geeky lab assistant at a time," he quipped.

"Someone has to." Gwenyth chuckled. "How's the K9 training going?"

"Apparently, I missed the memo about bringing a dog with me."

"Uh-oh."

"So I reached out to the head instructor, and

she's letting me test drive a potential new partner named Major."

"Are you serious?" Gwenyth gasped. "You're actually getting a dog?"

"Every super hero needs a sidekick."

"Pictures, please."

"Coming right up." He'd need to take a snapshot of Major first.

"I already liked you," Gwenyth said softly, "but a man with a dog is irresistible."

"I like the sound of that."

"The only real competition you have for my attention right now is Plant Zero."

"Guess I better hurry home!" He feigned alarm.

"Great idea!"

"Miss you." He pressed his lips to the receiver in a silent kiss, wishing he dared to tell her what was really on his heart. However, he didn't want to scare her away by dropping the L word on her this soon.

"Miss you, too. 'Night, Jett."

"'Night, babe." He disconnected the line and immediately missed the sound of her voice.

He knew it was a long time before he was actually going to see his bed again. He hadn't been kidding about putting in extra hours to get Major ready to join tomorrow's K9 training classes. Though the dog was well-trained, it would take time to earn his trust to the point where they could work together as well synchronized partners.

Jett paid a visit to the food and treat closet and filled one of his jeans pockets with doggie biscuits. Then he continued on down the aisle of the kennel.

This time, Major remained silent when Jett entered his cage. The dog was finished eating his dinner and was pacing the length of the cage in front of the concrete walkway. Jett quickly held up his phone, took a snapshot of Major, and sent it to Gwenyth.

"You want to go for a run, buddy?" Jett reached for the dog's leash, which was hanging from a hook affixed to the chain-link cage.

Major wagged his tail and barked.

"That sounded like a yes to me." Jett decided to test out a few commands on the dog before leaving the cage. "Watch me." It was the first command he'd learned in his dog training classes this week. He held a dog treat in front of Major's nose and drew it slowly toward his own face.

Major watched him steadily.

"Good boy." Jett gave him his first treat, which he gobbled up greedily. "Now, sit."

Major sat.

"You're making this way too easy on me, buddy." Jett gave him another treat and fastened Major's leash to his collar while he was stooped over the dog. "Come." He opened the cage door and led Major up the aisle.

Major didn't so much walk as prance.

"Why, you cocky thing, you," Jett chuckled. He took the dog inside the nearest gated playground. It was normally reserved for household pet training. He removed Major's leash. "Go stretch those legs."

Major took off running.

"I think you got yourself a dog, Channing."

He glanced up to find Deputy Snow leaning her elbows on the fence.

"Yeah." He folded his arms and watched the dog roll on the ground in the grass. "How much do I owe you?"

She snorted. "The late sheriff's wife donated Major to the police department, and they dropped him off here when he refused to leave his cage for three days straight."

"Can I at least make a donation to the school?"

She shrugged. "Tell you what, he's due for a checkup and a round of annual shots soon. If you want to make an appointment and have that taken care of before you leave town, I'll sign 'em over to you."

## CHAPTER 7: EXES AND OH'S

### GWENYTH

As the third week of Jett's absence stretched into the fourth, Gwenyth's brain conjured up all sorts of horrifying scenarios. Her relationship with Jett was far too new to take for granted. She imagined he was meeting dozens of amazing, accomplished women — fit and athletic ones. Women in law enforcement, women in forestry, women in uniform. How in heaven's name could a research scientist compete with all those glittering heroines?

Her life was full of far more mundane things like greenhouse visits, digging in soil, test tube experiments, and Echo Marcello.

"How's that hunky man of yours doing with all that puppy dog training?" Echo breezed through the office in a pair of hip-hugging black pants, matching platform boots, and a red leather jacket, looking her usual brand of marvelous.

"He adopted one." Feeling a bit guilty that she hadn't shared that bit of information yet, Gwenyth pulled up one of the many dog photos Jett had texted her. In this particular one, Major was completely airborne as he leaped up to grab something Jett had suspended over his head. Someone else must have snapped the picture of them.

Echo grabbed Gwenyth's wrist to hold the phone steady. "Be still my heart! Your man gets more swoony with each passing day."

"True, but he's been gone for weeks. According to the Book of Echo, that places me squarely in a dry spell," Gwenyth teased.

"No way. Nope. Nuh-uh!" Her assistant shook her head emphatically. "There's no such thing as a dry spell when you're dating a man like Jett Channing. You two have done nothing but text, call, and... apparently trade melt-your-heart doggie pictures the entire time he's been gone."

"It's not the same as him being here, though," Gwenyth sighed, "not even close. When he was in town, I was afraid things were going too fast. Now that he's gone, I'm afraid things will cool off too quickly."

"So keep the temperature soaring with big, sloppy phone kisses and...hold that thought. I just realized I might be getting the cart ahead of the horse here. Have you two even kissed yet?"

"Echo!" Gwenyth looked across her dark-rimmed glasses at her assistant with what she hoped was a solid you've-crossed-a-line look.

"Shut the front door!" Echo threw down the stack of folders she'd been holding and leaned on her desk with both hands to narrow her dark sparkling eyes at Gwenyth. "You've been holding out on me, haven't you?"

"We are so not having this conversation!" Blushing wildly, Gwenyth tried to duck behind her computer screen, but Echo wasn't near ready to let the topic go.

"Oh, come on! You can't just lay a bomb on me like that and quietly go back to typing lab reports. That's positively inhumane." Echo's hands flew to her head. "You gotta give me something here. I mean..." She threw her hands out dramatically, flashing her black lacquered fingertips in the air. "Was it a quick peck on the cheek or a full-on dive for tonsils?"

*It was...perfect.* Gwenyth felt her knees go weak at the memory. *Too much yet not enough.* For a kiss that was never supposed to happen, it had both terrified her and thrilled her. She'd lost track of where she ended and where he began when their mouths fused together.

"Wo-o-o-o-ow!" Echo whispered, hands remaining suspended in the air as she watched Gwenyth. "It was that good, huh?"

Gwenyth briefly closed her eyes and nodded. "It was earth-shattering and soul-shaking."

Echo made a moaning sound and slapped at the air with both hands. "Whew! Just hearing about your kiss has jolted me out of my own dry spell." She clacked her way around her desk, fanning her face. "I'm going to have to come up with some new material ASAP. Oh, honey!" She flopped in her chair just as the phone rang. Rolling her eyes at Gwenyth, she picked up the receiver and immediately started to scowl.

"John Rivers?" Her dark eyes rounded in alarm. She waved wildly to get Gwenyth's attention. "As in the Gator John show?"

Gwenyth froze in her chair. Why was her ex calling her at the office? She'd expected to hear from him again about, well, never!

"Holy mackerel! I love your show," Echo gushed, "All the alligators and water and...alligators. It's so nice meeting you over the phone! How can I help you, sir?" She paused and listened. "Ah. You're looking for Dr. Moore. Let me check and see if she's in her office." She balanced the phone on her shoulder, hastily scrawled a note on a sheet of paper, and held it up.

In large hot pink letters, it read, *Are you in a meeting?*

Gwenyth was temped to lie, but part of her was dying to know what this was about. Plus, if John

Rivers was anything, he was persistent. If he wanted to talk to her, he'd find a way. Might as well get it over with sooner rather than later.

She scrawled a note of her own and held it up. *Transfer him over.*

*No!* Echo mouthed, shaking her head violently.

*Yes,* Gwenyth mouthed back, bracing herself for another confrontation. Her breakup with John had been loud and painful, one in which John had accused her of not being supportive enough of his career and his show. He'd been furious about her accepting the position of department chair at Sam Houston State University, just as he was about to relocate his office headquarters to Corpus Christi.

"Well, what do you know? I found the lovely Dr. Moore. One sec while I transfer you." Echo's expression was less than thrilled as she viciously mashed a few buttons on her phone panel. "I hope you know what you're doing," she muttered.

*So do I.* Gwenyth picked up the phone. "Dr. Moore speaking."

"Gwen?" Gator John sounded so anxious that she sat forward in her chair.

"Is everything alright?"

"Of course it's not!" he bellowed so loudly that she had to hold the earpiece away for a few seconds. "You're there, and I'm all the way down here, a good four hours away. I think about you constantly. I know we had a big fight, sugar, but I wasn't expecting complete radio silence from you the past few weeks."

*What?* Gwenyth gripped the phone. They'd done more than fight. "We broke up, John, remember?" *You claimed you were going to start dating that super model, and I told you I hoped you both got eaten by alligators.*

"You know I didn't mean it," he protested. "I was just upset about you moving so far away. I think we can both agree we said things we regret."

*Actually, I wouldn't mind watching a gator take a snap at you on your show, but sure. I'm sorry we fought. I can give you that.* Gwenyth had always hated confrontations, whereas John seemed to thrive on them. He was forever taking a bite out of her after a bad day of work. Well, no more. She wasn't his to bark and snap at any longer. "What do you want from me, John?" The tone of their conversation was starting to alarm her.

"You!" he stated bluntly. "I want you back, Gwen."

*Well, you can't have me. I've already moved on.* Gwenyth blinked at the realization that it was true. Their rift had been a long time coming. She could see that now. They were two ships sailing in opposite directions, much farther apart in reality than the two hundred and seventy miles that currently separated them on paper. They wanted different things in life, such different things that there was no meeting in the middle.

"I am sorry we fought," he continued. "I am sorry for everything. This is me, taking it all back and asking — No! I'm begging for a do-over."

*I don't want your apologies! And no more do-overs!* She'd given him many of them in the past, and they never lasted long. *I just want to be left alone.*

"I am sorry for every angry word. Every unfair accusation." He paused. "Say something, Gwen. Please? I'm on my knees, sugar."

She seriously doubted his last statement. John had a penchant for drama. He was a showman, after all. More than likely, he was lounged behind his desk with his feet propped on the head of that goofy stuffed kangaroo he'd brought back from his latest trip to Australia.

"What about Yasmin?" she snapped.

"What about her, sweetheart?" he inquired tenderly. "Oh!" There was a rustling sound, as if he was sitting up straighter. "You thought I was serious about her?"

"I did get the impression you were dumping me for another woman, yes," she supplied coldly. *Are we through here?*

"Never happened," he assured, as if his adamant denial now would simply erase all his previous claims. "I was only trying to make you jealous.

Trying to give you a reason to turn down that blasted university job and move to Corpus Christi with me."

*Well, it didn't work.* "I love my job here at the university," she resented the way he was belittling it, as if it didn't matter, "and I'm not looking to rekindle things with you. I'm sorry, John, but it's over between us. You need to accept that."

At those words, Echo, who'd been staring at her in alarm, threw up her arms in the hallelujah sign.

Gwenyth rolled her eyes at her assistant.

"B-but—!" John sputtered.

"I'm seeing someone else," she interrupted.

"If you're trying to make me jealous, it's working," he growled. "I'm so jealous I can't see straight."

And there was the drama again. *I can't do this anymore.* "This is goodbye, John."

"But—"

"No, John. It's truly over this time. I wish you the best. Please don't call here again." She disconnected the line and sat there clutching the phone with shaking hands.

"Way to tell that bozo what's what, Dr. Moore!" Echo stood, clapping her hands.

Gwenyth tasted bitterness. "I can't believe he thought he could call with a half-hearted apology and just waltz right back into my life...again. What's his deal? I really thought it was over this time." She scowled at the phone.

Echo shook her head. "Classic ex move, if you

ask me. He saw you moving on with your life and wasn't happy about it. One of those I-don't-want-you-for-myself things, but I-don't-want-you-for-anyone-else, either."

"That's messed up," Gwenyth snapped.

"Right you are." Echo pointed her thumb and forefinger like a weapon. "Well, you put him nicely in his place. That was a hundred shades of impressive. To be honest, doctor, you're so nice that I wasn't sure you had it in you."

Gwenyth pressed a hand to her forehead, feeling like she had a fever. "What if he tries something?" she asked worriedly.

"What do you mean?" Echo cocked her head.

"Well, he's always been dramatic," Gwenyth sighed.

"No, seriously. What do you mean?" Echo demanded.

Gwenyth made a face. "He's a showman, that's what. An entertainer. He's been known to record crank calls and stage all sorts of things. I don't think there's any line he wouldn't cross if he thought it would raise his ratings."

Echo nodded grimly. "And there's Jett Channing in your life now. Unlimited amounts of opportunity to tap there."

"Right."

"Why are you holding your forehead? Are you sick?" Echo inquired anxiously.

"Just upset, I think." Gwenyth pulled up her electronic calendar on her desktop and scrolled through the next few days. "Listen, I know this is a bad time for me to be taking off work, but I really think I should go visit Jett this weekend." If she took off tomorrow, she could get the driving part out of the way and get herself settled into a hotel. That would leave her all day Saturday to plan a meet-up with Jett. Considering how rigorous and intense the Disaster City Search and Rescue Academy was purported to be, she had no idea what time would be best for Jett, especially on such short notice.

Echo pretended to hold a microphone to her mouth and sang out, "Dr. Moore is going to see her man!" She did a little jig in the middle of their office and came to a stand-still in front of Gwenyth's desk. "I totally approve this message." Her words were accompanied by a few head bobs.

Gwenyth flicked the capped end of her pen at one of her appointments flashing on the screen. "Dr. Carmichael from the University of Dallas isn't going to be happy about postponing our next planning meeting."

Echo spun around. "I gotcha covered, honey. This is the part where you let me work my magic. I'll show you exactly how I earned my moniker of best assistant in the universe."

FRIDAY WAS cool and overcast with a misting rain. Gwenyth shot an accusing look at the sky mid-morning as she tossed her overnight bag, laptop case, and purse into the passenger seat of her Porsche. "Can't you cut me any slack?" she grumbled. Driving in rain would only make the Friday traffic that much worse.

Borrowing from Echo's playbook, she'd opted to wear black skinny jeans, high-heeled boots, and a swanky lemon yellow shrug — minus the black nail polish, of course. She was happy with the result and hoped Jett would be, too, if he got to see her in them this evening. If not, she had another swanky outfit packed for tomorrow.

Her phone buzzed a few times with incoming messages. Gwenyth scanned the screen and grinned. It was Echo spam texting her one word at a time with a frantic sounding message in all caps .

PLEASE
DON'T
GO!!!
TROPICAL
STORM
HEADING
OUR
WAY!!!

The message was accompanied by three whole

lines of emojis — lightning strikes, rain clouds, umbrellas, and a dragon, of all things.

Before Gwenyth could respond, Echo was calling. Gwenyth accepted the call with a laugh. "What's with the dragon?"

"It was supposed to be an alligator, but I was in a hurry. I take it you read my emergency message?"

"In all caps, darling."

"Don't go! Don't go! Don't go!" Echo pleaded. "You can still take the day off, but go home and take sultry selfies to flood your man's inbox. Just please, please, please don't go driving into that tropical storm."

"The storm is south of us, my dear over-concerned coworker."

"And heading north at about forty-one miles per hour, according to the latest weather update."

"Well, good news." Gwenyth slid behind the wheel of her car and shut the door. "I rarely drive less than eighty."

"Did you just shut your car door?" Echo accused. "You open that thing right back up, Dr. Moore. You hear me?"

"Echo, I'm fine," Gwenyth started her engine, "and I'm going to continue being fine all the way to Dallas today and all the way back home from Dallas on Sunday. Save your worry-warting for a real emergency, okay?"

Echo moaned loudly. "I've got a really bad feeling about this."

"Grab another cup of coffee, my friend," Gwenyth instructed cheerfully. "That always works for me."

She could hear the murmur of voices in the background.

"Gotta go for now," Echo hissed into the mouthpiece, "but I am still not one bit happy about you making that drive today. You better call me with proof of life updates, every hour on the hour."

"Bye, Echo." Gwenyth chuckled and disconnected the line.

Echo rang her again a little over two hours into the drive. "Have you been on Twitter yet today?"

Gwenyth snorted. "I'm driving, and I'm just now working my way through my second cup of coffee. What do you think?"

"Awesome! Well, I was just making conversation." Echo's tone sounded a little off. "Actually, the real reason I was calling was about your meeting with Dr. Carmichael. He actually sounded relieved about postponing—"

"What's on Twitter, Echo?"

"Ah...not much. You know, the usual hashtag Friday Funday stuff..." she drawled in a tone that Gwenyth privately referred to as her *false cheer voice.* "About Dr. Carmichael's schedule—"

"What did he do, Echo?" Gwenyth gripped her steering wheel with both hands.

A crack of thunder made her jolt.

"Sheesh!" she muttered. A glance through the windshield up at the sky made her wince. It was getting ugly up there — all green slashes and dark smudges of purple. It was as if someone had spilled a few buckets of paint across the sky and then fallen in it.

"Man, that sounded close! Please assure me you didn't just get hit by lightning," Echo demanded nervously.

"I did not just get hit by lightning. I'm fine, but you're not going to be if you don't hurry up and spill what Gator John is up to today."

"Okay, okay," Echo growled. "He taped your conversation yesterday and replayed select parts of it on a video he posted to Youtube. He's been using hashtag #Gwator and begging you to take him back, and I really hate to admit this, but..." she gave a long-suffering sigh, "this one's going viral, honey."

"Gwator!" Gwenyth exclaimed.

"Yeah, it's your name mashed together with Gator. Most unfortunately, his fans are gobbling it up."

Another peal of thunder crashed around Gwenyth. The aftershocks sounded like a thousand and one plates shattering.

"Oh, my lands! That sounded closer than the last

one!" Echo exclaimed. "Are you driving through an intergalactic battle between alien clans or what?"

"I don't know, but I'm starting to get worried," Gwenyth confessed. "The sky looks really weird."

"Uh-huh. This is the part where you admit I was right and turn your little scientific butt around and get home where you belong."

"But I'm almost there!" Gwenyth protested. "Just take a look at the weather for me and see what I'm up against. Maybe you can help me navigate around it or something."

"Looking it up right now, and...no way!" her assistant gasped.

"Give it to me straight, Echo!" Gwenyth winced as the first oversized drops of rain pounded her car like watery fists.

"I don't understand." Her voice shook. "It's like the tropical storm heading your way had babies, and their babies had babies. What the bajeebers? There are clusters of storms swirling over the entire southern half of Texas!"

The rain pelted down harder, making it nearly impossible for Gwenyth to see. "Okay. Ah...as soon as I reach the next overpass, I'm pulling over to wait it out."

"Okay, honey. I'll just stay on the phone, in case you need anything."

Gwenyth bit her lower lip. She was very much in tune with Echo's many moods, and this one was scaring her. She was too calm and too deadpan, which mean she was truly afraid. "I can't see much of anything." Gwenyth turned her windshield wipers on high, but it didn't help. The rain was coming down too hard and too fast. "I should probably just pull over right here."

"Where is here?" Echo inquired in that same calm, deadpan voice.

"I'm on Highway 45, somewhere past Richland because I remember passing the reservoir about a half hour ago."

"Oo, yeah. You're right. You're almost there." Echo didn't sound the least bit happy about that fact.

Gwenyth slowly worked her way to the right shoulder. "I see a sign for...Highway 20." A mighty crash to her left interrupted her travel update.

"What was that?" Echo inquired sharply.

"I'm not sure," Gwenyth returned worriedly. She blinked as a flaming wheel rolled in her direction. The flames were quickly extinguished by the rain, and the tire bumped into the side of her car. "An accident, I think. There are tires on fire and everything."

"Oh, dear heavens!" Echo started praying softly beneath her breath.

Gwenyth wasn't sure if she'd made it all the way to the shoulder on the side of the road. It was too difficult to see through the storm, but she stopped her car, anyway. A loud squealing sounded, and she watched in horror as an enormous mangled piece of metal skidded in her direction. It took a few seconds for her to realize it wasn't just a piece of metal. It was a dark pickup truck, and it was headed straight for her.

"I'm about to be in an accident!" she shouted to Echo.

The impact jarred every bone in her body and sent her and her car hurtling into what felt like a free-fall.

"Help!" she screamed. "Please, God! Help!"

## CHAPTER 8: STORM FRONT

### JETT

Thunder rumbled and the power flashed on and off a few times, but the hard corps instructors of the Disaster City Search and Rescue Academy (DCSRA) continued on with their lesson plans as if nothing was amiss. Jett couldn't help being impressed with their unflinching dedication to their jobs. This afternoon, former Gunnery Sergeant Justin Ford and Officer John Lee were tag-teaming their way through a fascinating hands-on lab on the topic of tracking and scenting.

Though Jett and his classmates were sitting inside one of the conference rooms, they'd been allowed to bring their dogs with them to class. That was how the DCSRA operated. Too stormy to work outside? Fine! Bring the work inside.

Ford and Lee had set up a series of black boxes throughout the room to form a miniature obstacle course. The boxes had circular holes cut in the top, and they housed an array of different scents, thanks to the various socks and t-shirts his classmates had contributed to the exercise from their dirty laundry hampers. His and Major's turn was coming next. They would be required to track a "missing" classmate by following the trail of clues left behind via the items of laundry.

Jett's phone buzzed with an incoming message. At first, he tried to ignore it, knowing the use of personal electronic devices was highly discouraged during school hours, but it kept going off. Gritting his teeth in exasperation, he tried to discreetly peek at it while holding it half beneath the conference table in front of him.

*What the—?*

Someone was spamming his number one word at a time in all caps.

*GWENYTH*
*MOORE*
*IN*
*HORRIFIC*
*ACCIDENT.*
*CALL*
*ME*
*NOW!!!*
*—ECHO*
*MARCELLO*

Jett stared at the screen in disbelief. Echo was the name of Gwenyth's executive assistant. He'd never met her, but he'd heard quite a lot about her colorful personality. Nor did he know how she'd gotten ahold of his number. All that mattered was, she had.

He mashed the number at the top of the screen to dial her, half rising from his seat.

"Got something more important going on over there, Charming?" former Gunnery Sergeant Justin Ford paused his lecture to pin Jett with a cold-as-ice stare.

Jett grimaced. His celebrity status sure hadn't earned him any brownie points at this school. It had only made the instructors ride him ten times harder than his peers, or so it seemed to him. He'd embraced the challenge, though, giving the training at the academy everything he had to prove his number of followers on social media wouldn't distract him from his goal of becoming search and rescue certified.

"My girlfriend has been in a car accident, sergeant." Jett didn't have time to explain further before the phone started to ring. *Come on! Pick up! Pick up!*

"Jett!" Echo shouted into the earpiece. "Gwenyth was on her way to see you, but the weather turned really bad on her. Like freaking Armageddon. She said something about tires on fire and that she was about to be in an accident. Then she started screaming."

The air left Jett's chest in a suffocating huff. He dragged in a painstaking breath so he could speak. "Where is she?" he growled.

"Somewhere north of Richland. She saw a sign for Highway 20."

"That's less than ten miles from here! Was she driving her Porsche?"

"Yes. I tried to stop her from getting on the road, Jett. I really did, but she was all crazy worried about some stunt her ex pulled online this morning. I think she wanted to come explain things to you in person. He's trying to win her back, you see, and—"

"I gotta go, Echo." Jett didn't give a flying rat's tail what Gwenyth's ex was trying to stir up. She was his girl now.

"Call me when you find her. Please?" Echo begged.

"I promise!" He disconnected the line.

The power flashed off again in the conference room. This time it stayed off.

The DCSRA commander, a retired soldier with salt-and-pepper brown hair whom everyone lovingly referred to as Sarge, popped his head inside the door. "We're under a severe storm watch. You know the protocols." Just as quickly as he appeared, the commander was gone.

Jett met the gaze of the retired gunnery sergeant

who'd been particularly tough on him the past two weeks.

"You heard the commander, Charming." The man jammed a thumb in the direction of the rear exit.

"I'm not going to follow you to some storm shelter while my girlfriend is out there injured or...or worse." Jett glared at him in disbelief.

"Is that so? This isn't a pick-your-own ending kind of storybook, Charming." The fellow's voice was as dry as sawdust. "Like Sarge said, we have protocols around here."

"You know what?" Jett had endured enough of the man's sarcasm to last him a lifetime. "You can recommend me for expulsion when I get back. In the meantime, Major and I will be out there saving lives. Come on, little buddy!" He gave a sharp whistle that brought Major to his feet.

"You'd have never made much of a handler anyway with your hero complex," Ford shouted after him. "You can't perform search and rescue ops if you don't respect the authorities who have jurisdiction over you."

Jett froze in his tracks and pivoted to face the fool. "We are the authorities!" he snarled. With that, he slammed out of the room and stormed from the building, seething at the man's utter lack of humanity. No real man would've ever asked him to sit on his hands while his girlfriend was stranded out there in a storm.

Rain sheeted down on him and Major, drenching them in seconds, as they made their way to the parking lot.

"Wait up, Channing!" a man shouted.

Jett increased his pace, refusing to turn around. Nobody and their army were going to keep him from going after his girl. He mashed the button on his remote ignition switch, and the Land Rover purred to life.

He bounded forward a few more strides and flung open the door. Major bounded inside the vehicle ahead of him and claimed the passenger seat. Just as he released the emergency brake, the right passenger door opened and a tall, hulking creature hurled himself inside.

In a flash, Jett retrieved the pistol he carried in his glove compartment and trained it on the intruder.

The dark features of Officer John Lee stared back. "Whoa, there!" He threw up his hands.

"Get out!" Jett roared. "I'm not going back."

"Neither am I," John returned mildly. "I'm coming along to help you find your girlfriend."

"Huh." *Really?* Jett tossed his piece back in the glove compartment and slammed it shut. He threw the Land Rover in reverse and spun out of the parking lot. "What about your precious protocols, officer?"

"What about them, Channing? I think you can guess where my priorities lie from where I'm sitting right now."

Jett met his instructor's gaze in the rearview mirror. "You do realize Sergeant Ford has every intention of drumming me out of the academy when I return."

"He can try." Officer Lee didn't sound too worried. "My presence here in the car might make that a little harder."

"Well...thanks." Jett returned his attention to the road, which was getting harder and harder to see. Vehicles were parked everywhere, some right in the middle of the street, as if the drivers were terrified to keep going.

"Welcome." John Lee leaned between the two front seats, pointing and calling out obstacles for Jett to maneuver around. "I did some checking up on you, Channing, and I'm not just referring to your Twitter account."

"Oh?"

His long dark arm shot out. "Box in the road!"

Jett swung wide to avoid it.

"Yeah, I wanted to understand why a former bodybuilding champion would choose a second career as a forest ranger."

"And?" Jett wasn't sure why the man's opinion mattered, but it did. A lot. He respected Officer Lee enormously.

"Found out about your rising role in the Atakapa-Ishak tribe, for one thing."

Jett shrugged and swerved around a red Volkswagen that was sitting in the middle of an intersection. "Our application for tribal status has been turned down in two states so far." There were reasons for it. The process was a complicated one, and not everyone in tribal leadership positions understood how to wade through so much governmental red tape.

"So turn in another application." There was a smile in Officer Lee's voice.

"Already have," Jett snapped.

"Figured that." The officer pointed again. "Truck!"

Jett swerved his way down the entrance ramp of the freeway. *I'm coming, Gwenyth! Hang on just a little longer, babe.*

"Then there was that whole impromptu rescue op with that pretty scientist a few weeks ago."

"She's my girlfriend now." Jett knew he was bragging, but he didn't care. Gwenyth was worth bragging about. She was brilliant, gorgeous, and — Lord willing — still alive. "Help me find her, God."

"You a man of faith?" Officer Lee inquired, sounding surprised.

"What? Oh." Jett realized he must have spoken his prayer aloud. He'd not been much of a church goer in the past but... "I think I started believing in miracles the day I met Dr. Gwenyth Moore."

"Wow!"

"Yeah. If I had to sum her up in one word, *wow* would be it."

"Well, I can't wait to meet her," Officer Lee assured warmly. "The last reason I decided to stick my neck out for you was because I contacted one of my former academy classmates, Deputy Amber Snow. She gave me the rundown about how you got Major here to start eating and living again."

Major woofed at the sound of his name.

Officer Lee's dark arm shot out again. "Person!"

Jett jammed on his brakes, knowing they had to be getting close to the site of the accident. He leaped from his SUV and approached the man. "Are you alright, sir?"

The man spun dizzily around to face him. Red was oozing from a cut on his forehead. "My truck." He pointed to the side of the road, though Jett could see nothing there. "I hit a car, but I managed to get out before they both rolled over the embankment."

Jett's blood turned icy in his veins. "Was it a silver Porsche that you hit?"

The man stared at him, uncomprehending.

"I've got 'em." Officer Lee helped heft the man inside one of the back passenger seats to examine his head injury.

Jett's head swung from side to side as he swiftly

scanned the scene of the accident. There were two tires lying in the middle of the road.

*Tires on fire*, Echo had said. His gut told him he was in the right spot.

He whistled for Major to follow him, and together they approached the side of the road. It wasn't as steep as a textbook definition of a cliff, but the sides of the hill were rocky and spanned a distance that was roughly the size of a basketball court. Though the rain was still falling hard and fast, Jett could make out a mangled looking shape at the bottom of the hill.

"I'm going down there!" he shouted to Officer Lee.

"Be right behind you!"

"Gonna need you up high with the ropes," he shouted back.

"Roger that!"

Confident that Officer Lee would be of assistance during his ascent, Jett slipped and slid his way down the rocky incline with Major yipping at his heels. He took a few bumps and scrapes on the way down, but he barely felt them. He approached the mangled metal and noted the silver paint.

"Gwenyth!" he cried. "Gwenyth! Are you in there?" *Answer me, babe.* The bumper to the truck was laying a few feet away, crumpled like a used tissue. Broken glass was strewn everywhere.

"Gwenyth!" Jett couldn't remember ever feeling

this frantic. A sick taste pooled on his tongue at what he might find behind all that crunched up metal. He reached the Porsche and yanked with all his might at the crumpled door. To his shock, the whole thing came off in his hands. He threw it aside to peer into the vehicle. It was empty.

*Oh, dear God!* Visions of her being thrown or pinned filled his brain, making him sway on his feet.

Major gave a sobbing squeal and pushed his muzzle against the damp leg of Jett's jeans.

*Right.* The dog needed a scent in order to assist in the search. Jett dragged in a few lungfuls of air and slapped at his pockets in frustration. He hadn't been dating Gwenyth long enough to accumulate a stash of hair ties or forgotten cardigans. The only thing he had that belonged to her was... "Her business card!" he rasped. He had her business card — one that smelled like her perfume. He knew it, because he'd foolishly sniffed it more than once since they'd been apart. It wasn't much, but it was better than nothing and it should be relatively dry since it was tucked inside his wallet.

He dug for it, stooping over so his body would protect it from the rain. "Here, boy." He guided Major's snout to the precious article, praying it would be enough.

Major barked and snuffled along the ground as he made his way around the site of the accident.

As a precaution, Jett returned the business card

to his wallet and pocketed it, in the event Major needed a second run at it. He cupped his hands over his mouth. "Gwenyth!" He shouted her name again and again.

The rain subsided to a light drizzle, and Officer Lee's face appeared at the top of the hill. "Any luck?" he called down.

Jett raised and lowered his hands helplessly. Gwenyth's absence made no sense. This was her car. Then again, until he located a body, he could hang on to his ever-thinning thread of hope that she was still alive.

Major suddenly pivoted and ran back up the hill, barking madly. However, he didn't retrace their exact steps. He ran in a diagonal line and stopped about halfway up the hill. He stood there and continued to bark.

Jett shaded his eyes against the sun that was starting to creep out from behind the clouds. *What is it, Major? What did you find, buddy?* It appeared to be some sort of outcropping of rock wedged behind a twist of vines.

He slipped and slid his way over the glassy wet rocks to determine what his dog had found. Pushing aside the sodden vines, he stared for a moment, then slid weakly to his knees.

"You're alive!" He caught his breath on a sob as he took in Gwenyth's mud-streaked face and torn clothing. "Are you..." He tenderly reached out to push a strand of brilliant red hair from her eyes. "Tell me where it hurts, babe." He feared the worst — a broken back or neck, internal bleeding, and the like.

"Everywhere," she groaned, struggling to sit up.

"Don't move," he pleaded. He glanced up in Officer Lee's direction. "I found her!" he shouted. "Call an ambulance." As soon as the words left his mouth, he realized how foolish they sounded. It wasn't likely an ambulance would be able to reach them any time soon. No doubt there were hundreds of other 911 calls in the queue.

"I'm okay, Jett. Really, I am."

"You don't know that," he protested. "The accident," he choked and was unable to continue. He wasn't certain how she'd ever made it out of that twist of metal below, much less how she'd managed to crawl halfway up the hill.

"I got out just in time," she said softly. "When I realized my car was going over, I threw open the door and jumped. This is where I landed."

Jett closed his eyes for a moment, weak with relief at the knowledge that Gwenyth had narrowly cheated death yet again. "You're like a cat with nine lives," he said in wonder, reaching for her and gathering her close.

She reached back, twining her arms around his neck. "This is *not* the grand entrance I planned to make into Dallas."

"I bet." He pressed his face to her neck, soaking

up her warmth, vitality, and the unique presence that was simply her.

"I wanted to surprise you." She tangled her fingers in his hair with her good hand.

"You succeeded."

She gave a damp laugh. "How did you find me?"

"Echo." He pressed tiny kisses against her neck, earlobe, and temple.

"Of course." Gwenyth chuckled. "Still living up to her best-assistant-in-the-universe reputation." She gave him a tight hug. "How did you get away from the academy? I thought they pretty much kept you in balls and chains there."

"They tried," Jett disclosed grimly, "and failed." He claimed her mouth at last. "There is nothing," he declared between kisses, "nothing that could have kept me away once I realized you needed me."

He tasted hope, joy, and something else that took his breath away.

"I love you, Jett!" Tears streamed down her cheeks as she kissed him back. "I love you so much."

His heart pounded like thunder at her admission. He'd never — not in all his wildest daydreaming — thought she would be the one to confess her feelings first.

"I love you more," he declared huskily, claiming her mouth in a way that left no doubt where he stood on the matter. His lips roved over hers, cherishing and tender. He never wanted to stop kissing her.

Whatever had held her back the first time he tried to kiss her was gone. She was his now, truly his.

"That's not possible." She cupped his cheek.

He reveled in the adoration he read in her gaze. "Yes, it is. Marry me, Gwenyth." He hadn't expected to propose to her on the side of a craggy hill, but the moment felt right.

Her smile slipped, and the rosy blush staining her cheeks faded. "What if the cancer comes back, Jett?"

He gazed deeply into her eyes, his heart clenching with determination. "We'll fight it together." With every last penny and resource he possessed.

"And what if I can't have children? I took a lot of radiation as a kid."

Jett nuzzled the side of her face. "You already told me you wanted to adopt a pack of dogs. I don't think Major will mind the company."

As if on cue, Major butted his head against Jett's shoulder.

She smiled through a fresh round of tears. "What if—?"

He sealed his mouth over hers to shut her up. It was a good while before he spoke again. "What if you just say yes?"

"Yes," she whispered.

He gazed at her in joy and wonder. *She said yes. She actually said yes!*

A helicopter rumbled overhead, making Gwenyth rock back in Jett's arms so she could tip her face upward.

He took the opportunity to kiss the exposed skin of her throat.

"Seriously?" she groaned. "You're not going to believe this, Jett, but I think the paparazzi has tracked us down. Again."

"Welcome to my world, babe."

She jolted in his arms. "There's a man up there!" she gasped.

Jett swiveled around to take a look. "That's Officer John Lee, one of my instructors."

Officer Lee jogged along the crest of the hill to reach the point directly above them. He tossed down one end from a coil of rope. "Make it look good for the cameras, folks!"

## CHAPTER 9: FINDING TOGETHER

### GWENYTH

***Twenty-four hours later***

"Oh. My. Gawsh!" Echo Marcello gave an excited bounce in the middle of the spare bed on the opposite side of Gwenyth's hotel room. She'd spent nearly all night on the road, against the advisory of law enforcement officials between Houston and Dallas. It had taken that long for her to skirt past all the carnage left by the storm.

She turned snapping dark eyes to Gwenyth. "Did you see that headline scrolling at the bottom of the screen?" She had flipped on a news station in her perennial hunt for the juiciest bits of gossip. But she'd mostly been watching the many glowing accounts of Jett Channing's latest heroics.

"Sorry, I missed it." Gwenyth was flooded with happiness just watching her assistant look so happy. Goodness! Assistant didn't even begin to describe what Echo had become to Gwenyth. The two women were way beyond the employer-employee relationship at this point. They were true friends. No, it was even more than that. They were like sisters.

"Well, lucky you. Here it comes again." Echo gestured imperiously at the screen with the narrow black remote.

Gwenyth took one look and laughed.

It read: *The Rebound Rescue.*

The willowy blonde newscaster flashed a picture on the screen, depicting Gator John's heinous attempt to boost his ratings with his whole #Gwator campaign.

*"In a bid to win back his ex-girlfriend, TV host Gator John has been tweeting sweet and humorous apologies to the enormous entertainment of his many followers,"* the newscaster said laughingly, *"but it looks like former bodybuilding champion Jett Channing was the one who saved the day and the girl with a daring hillside rescue during yesterday's cluster of tropical storms. Once fans caught wind of the rivalry between these two men in their race to win one woman's heart, they started calling Jett Channing's heroic act The Rebound Rescue, a story that has since gone viral."* The newscaster paused and turned to her fellow Channel 9 anchor. *"I don't know about you, Mike, but my bet's on the forest ranger for this one. Who's getting your vote?"*

"I can't understand why you keep watching that stuff." Gwenyth slid her legs over the side of her bed.

Echo giggled. "Maybe because they always seem to work their way up to sweaty pics of your man working out in the gym?"

"Just stop already!"

"Oh, come on! Dry spell, remember?" But Echo obligingly switched the channel. "You have nothing to worry about. Trust me. You've got Jett so flamboozled with your awesomeness, his brain doesn't even register the existence of other living creatures when you're in the room." Her face took on an arrested expression for a second. Then she tipped back her head and howled at something happening on the screen.

Gwenyth frowned and glanced at the television. "Cartoons? Honestly, Echo! What are you? Six?"

Echo's lips parted in surprise. "Girl, that must be all the scrapes and bruises talking over there, because this show is freaking hilarious. All I need is popcorn to go with it." She mimed tossing a piece of popcorn in the air and catching it with her mouth. "Mind if I order room service while you and your man *jet* out on your date?" She winked at Gwenyth. "Pun intended!" She made a ka-ching motion with her arm.

Rolling her eyes, Gwenyth padded her way to the dressing mirror around the corner. "Ow, ow, ow!"

she yelped as each step seemed to jar another ache or pain.

"Aw, sweetie!" Echo leaped out of bed with her black kimono flowing behind her like a superhero cape. "I know you've been through a lot. Here." She rummaged through her oversized suitcase that appeared to be jammed with everything known to man.

Gwenyth peeked around the corner and shook her head. Unless she was mistaken, there was even a jar of peanut butter poking its lid from the top of the hodge-podge.

"Aha!" Echo twirled around, making her black kimono swirl around her pale legs. She held out a small glass cylinder. "It's the test-tube version, but I — the most extraordinarily accomplished executive assistant on the planet — extracted some of those marvelous antioxidants from one of your hybrid plants in the greenhouse."

"You didn't." Gwenyth couldn't have been more touched...or pleased.

"Oh, I did!" Echo danced the test tube across the room in Gwenyth's direction.

"Here and I was about to settle for a regular ol' Tylenol." Gwenyth swiped the test tube from her friend, uncapped it, and gave it an experimental sniff. "What's it suspended in?"

"Nothing." Echo tossed back her long dark hair with an innocent expression. "Just a little something

I call my happy juice." She gave a preening smile and clapped her hands in front of her chin. "Try it already!"

"Happy juice?" Gwenyth arched her brows. "I'm more of an organic, wholistic, non-alcohol kind of girl."

"Where's the trust?" Echo made a face at her. "I assure you, my concoction checks all those boxes, honey." She pressed a hand to her heart. "Now drink up."

With a sigh of misgiving that was laced with curiosity, Gwenyth tipped up the test tube. Her eyes widened. It was quite possibly the most delicious thing she'd ever tasted. "That's amazing, Echo. What is it?"

Echo flushed with pleasure. "That, my dear Dr. Moore, is how we are going to sell your miracle medicine to the American public and then to the rest of the world."

"You may be on to something there, partner."

A knock sounded on the door.

"That's Jett, and I'm way too sore to go hunting for my shoes," Gwenyth hissed in alarm to Echo.

"I gotcha, girlie." Her assistant dove in the closet for Gwenyth's heels and knelt down to assist her in donning them.

"Just like Cinderella. Thank you!" Gwenyth sighed. The soft cast remaining on her wrist had additionally rendered it difficult to do much with her hair or makeup, so Echo had come to her rescue in those areas, as well.

Her red hair was cascading over her bare shoulders in an impossible tumble of waves, since Echo had talked her into wearing a strapless emerald-hued evening gown. She'd somehow managed to fetch it from Gwenyth's condo before departing for Dallas.

"Are you sure the gown isn't too much?" Gwenyth asked anxiously, taking one last peek at herself in the mirror.

"Uh, this is Jett Channing we're talking about." Echo made a face at her in the mirror. "I guarantee wherever that man is taking you tonight is over-the-top nice."

"I just—"

"No more buts." Echo held up a hand that was, for once, painted with sparkly blue nail polish instead of black. "You're perfect, and I'm out of here. Go be happy with your man." With that, she promptly shut herself inside the bathroom and turned on the ceiling fan, presumably to give them a bit of privacy.

Drawing in a bracing breath, Gwenyth opened the door of her hotel room. And promptly forgot how to breathe.

Jett was wearing a black tuxedo with a showy white shirt. His dark wavy hair was slicked back, and his gaze caressed her with an intensity that made her knees weak.

"You look amazing." He removed his hand from behind his back and produced a spray of red rosettes.

"So do you." Oblivious to the open door, Gwenyth stepped into his embrace.

His mouth brushed tenderly over hers, but he lifted his head all too soon. "Let's get out of here, shall we?" Excitement lit his features.

"Where are we going?" She desperately wanted to spend time with him, but she wasn't feeling up to a night on the town.

"Not far, babe." He whisked her into an elevator down the hall. They got off a few floors up where he whisked her into a second elevator. This one had a glass wall with a view of the city skyline and required him to punch a special code into a keypad to continue on.

"What a view!" Gwenyth rested her head on his shoulder as they ascended.

"I couldn't agree more," he said softly against her temple.

The elevator took them all the way to the top floor and higher. To Gwenyth's surprise, they disembarked on a glass-domed rooftop, similar to the one above Jett's penthouse. Stringed instruments were playing faintly in the background, and a small round table tumbling with white roses anchored the center of the room.

"Now, where were we?" Jett took her in his arms

again. "Oh, wait. I remember." His mouth descended on hers.

Gwenyth forgot all the horrors of the storm and the scrapes and bruises riddling her frame.

Jett's kisses were tender, his touch cherishing. "I love you, babe," he declared huskily against her lips.

"I love you, too, Jett," she sighed, then caught her breath when he slowly took a knee in front of her.

"I can't wait to make you my Mrs. Gwenyth Channing." He flipped open the lid of a small black box, and a white princess cut diamond flashed fire up at her. "Will you wear this for me?"

Her voice seemed to have disappeared, so she wordlessly held out her left hand, thankful it wasn't the one wearing a cast.

"It belonged to my mother," he explained. "I had it shipped here about a week ago from a safe deposit box in Los Angeles, hoping that sometime soon..." He gazed up at her with his heart in his eyes. "Then you showed up here in Dallas."

She gave a shaky laugh. "Sorry about the dramatic entrance."

"Par for the course," he teased, rising to take her in his arms once more, "considering how you already took my heart by storm."

She gave him a dreamy smile. "Speaking of storms, how are things going for you at the academy? Believe it or not, this weekend was originally supposed to be all about you."

"It's ah..." He nodded. "It's been interesting."

"Uh-oh."

"Yeah. Had one instructor in particular really riding my case the past two weeks. Turns out it was just part of the training. Apparently, they like to play good cop, bad cop here to turn up the heat and see how we'll perform under pressure."

"It actually sounds like pretty decent training."

"It is." He nodded. "That's why they make the big bucks." He glanced away for a few seconds.

"What is it, Jett?" She smoothed a hand over his lapel.

"Officer Lee, the guy you met at the scene of the accident, said he wants to recommend me for an instructor position at some point."

"Oh, wow!" Her eyes widened. "That would be here in Dallas, I suppose?"

"Not right away, but maybe in a couple of years. I need to gain more experience first, but he said I had the traits they were looking for when it comes time to expand their team."

"That's wonderful, Jett! Sounds like he has an enormous amount of confidence in your abilities. Why don't you seem happy about it?"

"I am," he assured with a frown, "I just want to be clear about something up front. Any decisions we make about jobs in the future, I'd like to make together. You and me." He brushed a finger down her cheek. "I don't want a long distance relationship.

Not now and not after we're married. I want to be with you — always."

"That's what I want, too." She stood on her tiptoes and lifted her face to his so they could seal their promise to each other with a kiss.

<<< THE END >>>

*I hope you enjoyed* **The Rebound Rescue***!*
*Keep turning for a sneak peek at*
**The Plus One Rescue***.*

*Much love,*
*Jo*

## SNEAK PREVIEW: THE PLUS ONE RESCUE

With a heroic-sounding name like his, Axel Hammerstone naturally made all the "most likely to succeed" lists in his high school yearbook. So it comes as no surprise to his friends when their favorite defensive tackle player returns from Afghanistan with a Purple Heart for an injury sustained while saving a bunch of fellow soldiers during an ambush. He's the only one who blames himself for the one man he failed to rescue during the ensuing explosion. Despite his own injuries, he's determined to atone for the loss of his best friend and battle buddy by devoting the rest of his career to search and rescue operations.

Kristi Kimiko was first called the "dog whisperer" on her sixteenth birthday when she coaxed a wounded Boston Terrier from their burning apartment complex. Seven years later, she's living her dream as an expert search and rescue trainer in Disaster City, Texas. Unfortunately, it leaves her little time for dating or any sort of social life, for that matter. When the hunky Axel half-limps and half-swaggers his way into her renowned dog training course with his beautiful golden retriever, she senses her life is about to change — especially after he somehow manages to coax her into serving as his Plus One at a big family birthday bash the following weekend.

If she's learned anything in her line of work, where there's smoke, there's a fire; and this particular hunky firefighter has a way of making the sparks fly every time he looks in her direction!

Step into the world of **Disaster City Search and Rescue**, where officers, firefighters, military, and medics, train and work alongside each other with the dogs they love, to do the most dangerous job of all — help lost and injured victims find their way home.

### The Plus One Rescue

*is available in eBook and paperback on Amazon + FREE in Kindle Unlimited!*

*Much love,*
*Jo*

## SNEAK PREVIEW: HER BILLIONAIRE BOSS

Jacey Maddox didn't bother straightening her navy pencil skirt or smoothing her hand over the sleek lines of her creamy silk blouse. She already knew she looked her best. She knew her makeup was flawless, each dash of color accentuating her sun kissed skin and classical features. She knew this, because she'd spent way too many of her twenty-five years facing the paparazzi; and after her trust fund had run dry, posing for an occasional glossy centerfold — something she wasn't entirely proud of.

Unfortunately, not one drop of that experience lent her any confidence as she mounted the cold, marble stairs of Genesis & Sons. It towered more than twenty stories over the Alaskan Gulf waters, a stalwart high-rise of white and gray stone with tinted windows, a fortress that housed one of the world's most brilliant think tanks. For generations, the sons of Genesis had ridden the cutting edge of industrial design, developing the concepts behind some of the nation's most profitable inventions, products, and manufacturing processes.

It was the one place on earth she was least welcome.

Not just because of how many of her escapades had hit the presses during her rebel teen years. Not just because she'd possessed the audacity to marry their youngest son against their wishes. Not just because she had encouraged him to pursue his dreams instead of their hallowed corporate mission — a decision that had ultimately gotten him killed. No. The biggest reason Genesis & Sons hated her was because of her last name. The one piece of herself she'd refused to give up when she'd married Easton Calcagni.

Maddox.

The name might as well have been stamped across her forehead like the mark of the beast, as she moved into the crosshairs of their first security camera. It flashed an intermittent red warning light and gave a low electronic whirring sound as it swiveled to direct its lens on her.

Her palms grew damp and her breathing quickened as she stepped into the entry foyer of her family's greatest corporate rival.

Recessed mahogany panels lined the walls above a mosaic tiled floor, and an intricately carved booth anchored the center of the room. A woman with silver hair waving past her shoulders lowered her reading glasses to dangle from a pearlized chain. "May I help you?"

Jacey's heartbeat stuttered and resumed at a much faster pace. The woman was no ordinary receptionist. Her arresting blue gaze and porcelain features had graced the tabloids for years. She was Waverly, matriarch of the Calcagni family, grand-mother to the three surviving Calcagni brothers. She was the one who'd voiced the greatest protests to Easton's elopement. She'd also wept in silence throughout his interment into the family mausoleum, while Jacey had stood at the edge of their gathering, dry-eyed and numb of soul behind a lacy veil.

The funeral had taken place exactly two months earlier.

"I have a one o'clock appointment with Mr. Luca Calcagni."

Waverly's gaze narrowed to twin icy points. "Not just any appointment, Ms. Maddox. You are here for an interview, I believe?"

Time to don her boxing gloves. "Yes." She could feel the veins pulsing through her temples now. She'd prepared for a rigorous cross-examination but had not expected it to begin in the entry foyer.

"Why are you really here?"

Five simple words, yet they carried the force of a full frontal attack. Beneath the myriad of accusations shooting from Waverly's eyes, she wanted to spin on her peep-toe stiletto pumps and run. Instead, she focused on regulating her breathing. It was a fair question. Her late husband's laughing face swam before her, both taunting and encouraging, as her mind ran over all the responses she'd rehearsed. None of them seemed adequate.

"I'm here because of Easton." It was the truth stripped of every excuse. She was here to atone for her debt to the family she'd wronged.

Pain lanced through the aging woman's gaze, twisting her fine-boned features with lines. Raw fury followed. "Do you want something from us, Ms. Maddox?" Condescension infused her drawling alto.

*Not what you're thinking, that's for sure. I'm no gold-digger.* "Yes. Very much. I want a job at Genesis." She could never restore Easton to his family, but she would offer herself in his place. She would spend the rest of her career serving their company in whatever capacity they would permit. It was the penance she'd chosen for herself.

The muscles around Waverly's mouth tightened a few degrees more. "Why not return to DRAW Corporation? To your own family?"

She refused to drop the elder woman's gaze as she absorbed each question, knowing they were shot like bullets to shatter her resolve, to remind her how unwelcome her presence was. She'd expected no other reception from the Calcagni dynasty; some would even argue she deserved this woman's scorn. However, she'd never been easily intimidated, a trait that was at times a strength and other times a curse. "With all due respect, Mrs. Calcagni, this *is* my family now."

Waverly's lips parted as if she would protest. Something akin to fear joined the choleric emotions churning across her countenance. She clamped her lips together, while her chest rose and fell several times. "You may take a seat now." She waved a heavily be-ringed hand to indicate the lounge area to her right. Lips pursed the skin around her mouth into papery creases, as she punched a few buttons on the call panel. "Ms. Maddox has arrived." Her frigid tone transformed each word into ice picks.

Jacey expelled the two painful clumps of air her lungs had been holding prisoner in a silent, drawn-out whoosh as she eased past the reception booth. She'd survived the first round of interrogations, a small triumph that yielded her no satisfaction. She knew the worst was yet to come. Waverly Calcagni was no more than a guard dog; Luca Calcagni was the one they sent into the boxing ring to finish off their opponents.

Luca apparently saw fit to allow her to marinate in her uneasiness past their appointment time. Not a surprise. He had the upper hand today and would do everything in his power to squash her with it. A full hour cranked away on the complicated maze of copper gears and chains on the wall. There was nothing ordinary about the interior of Genesis & Sons. Even their clocks were remarkable feats of architecture.

"Ms. Maddox? Mr. Calcagni is ready to see you."

She had to remind herself to breathe as she stood. At first she could see nothing but Luca's tall silhouette in the shadowed archway leading to the inner sanctum of Genesis & Sons. Then he took a step forward into a beam of sunlight and beckoned her to follow him. She stopped breathing again but somehow forced her feet to move in his direction.

He was everything she remembered and more from their few brief encounters. Much more. Up close, he seemed taller, broader, infinitely more intimidating, and so wickedly gorgeous it made her dizzy. That her parents had labeled him and his brothers as forbidden fruit made them all the more appealing to her during her teen years. It took her fascinated brain less than five seconds to recognize Luca had lost none of his allure.

The blue-black sheen of his hair, clipped short on the sides and longer on top, lent a deceptive innocence that didn't fool her one bit. Nor did the errant lock slipping to his forehead on one side. The expensive weave of his suit and complex twists of his tie far better illustrated his famed unpredictable temperament. His movements were controlled but fluid, bringing to her mind the restless prowl of a panther

as she followed him down the hall and into an elevator. It shimmered with mirrored glass and recessed
mahogany panels.

They rode in tense silence to the top floor.

Arrogance rolled off him from his crisply pressed
white shirt, to his winking diamond and white gold
cuff links, down to his designer leather shoes. In
some ways, his arrogance was understandable. He
guided the helm of one of the world's most profitable
companies, after all. And his eyes! They were as
beautiful and dangerous as the rest of him. Tawny
with flecks of gold, they regarded her with open
contempt as he ushered her from the elevator.

They entered a room surrounded by glass. One
wall of windows overlooked the gulf waters. The
other three framed varying angles of the Anchorage
skyline. Gone was the old-world elegance of the first
floor. This room was all Luca. A statement of power
in chrome and glass. Sheer contemporary mini-
malism with no frills.

"Have a seat." It was an order, not an offer. A call
to battle.

It was a battle she planned to win. She didn't
want to consider the alternative — slinking back to
her humble apartment in defeat.

He flicked one darkly tanned hand at the pair of
Chinese Chippendale chairs resting before his
expansive chrome desk. The chairs were stained
black like the heart of their owner. No cushions.

They were not designed for comfort, only as a place to park guests whom the CEO did not intend to linger.

She planned to change his mind on that subject before her allotted hour was up. "Thank you." Without hesitation, she took the chair on the right, making no pretense of being in the driver's seat. This was his domain. Given the chance, she planned to mold herself into the indispensable right hand to whoever in the firm he was willing to assign her. On paper, she might not look like she had much to offer, but there was a whole pack of demons driving her. An asset he wouldn't hesitate to exploit once he recognized their unique value. Or so she hoped.

To her surprise, he didn't seat himself behind his executive throne. Instead, he positioned himself between her and his desk, hiking one hip on the edge and folding his arms. It was a deliberate invasion of her personal space with all six feet two of his darkly arresting half-Hispanic features and commanding presence.

Most women would have swooned.

Jacey wasn't most women. She refused to give him the satisfaction of either fidgeting or being the first to break the silence. Silence was a powerful weapon, something she'd learned at the knees of her parents. Prepared to use whatever it took to get what she'd come for, she allowed it to stretch well past the point of politeness.

Luca finally unfolded his arms and reached for the file sitting on the edge of his desk. "I read your application and resume. It didn't take long."

According to her mental tally, the first point belonged to her. She nodded to acknowledge his insult and await the next.

He dangled her file above the trash canister beside his desk and released it. It dropped and settled with a papery flutter.

"I fail to see how singing in nightclubs the past five years qualifies you for any position at Genesis & Sons."

The attack was so predictable she wanted to smile, but didn't dare. Too much was at stake. She'd made the mistake of taunting him with a smile once before. Nine years earlier. Hopefully, he'd long forgotten the ill-advised lark.

Or not. His golden gaze fixed itself with such intensity on her mouth that her insides quaked with uneasiness. Nine years later, he'd become harder and exponentially more ruthless. She'd be wise to remember it.

"Singing is one of art's most beautiful forms," she countered softly. "According to recent studies, scientists believe it releases endorphins and oxytocin while reducing cortisol." *There.* He wasn't the only one who'd been raised in a tank swimming with intellectual minds.

The tightening of his jaw was the only indication

her answer had caught him by surprise. Luca was a man of facts and numbers. Her answer couldn't have possibly displeased him, yet his upper lip curled. "If you came to sing for me, Ms. Maddox, I'm all ears."

The smile burgeoning inside her mouth vanished. Every note of music in her had died with her husband. That part of her life was over. "We both know I did not submit my employment application in the hopes of landing a singing audition." She started to rise, a calculated risk. "If you don't have any interest in conducting the interview you agreed to, I'll just excuse my—"

"Have a seat, Ms. Maddox." Her veiled suggestion of his inability to keep his word clearly stung.

She sat.

"Remind me what other qualifications you disclosed on your application. There were so few, they seem to have slipped my mind."

Nothing slipped his mind. She would bet all the money she no longer possessed on it. "A little forgetfulness is understandable, Mr. Calcagni. You're a very busy man."

Her dig hit home. This time the clench of his jaw was more perceptible.

Now that she had his full attention, she plunged on. "My strengths are in behind-the-scenes marketing as well as personal presentations. As you are well aware, I cut my teeth on DRAW Corporation's drafting tables. I'm proficient in an exhaustive list of software programs and a whiz at compiling slides, notes, memes, video clips, animated graphics, and most types of printed materials. My family just this morning offered to return me to my former position in marketing."

"Why would they do that?"

"They hoped to crown me Vice President of Communications in the next year or two. I believe their exact words were *it's my rightful place.*" As much as she tried to mask it, a hint of derision crept in her voice. There were plenty of employees on her family's staff who were far more qualified and deserving of the promotion.

His lynx eyes narrowed to slits. "You speak in the past tense, Ms. Maddox. After recalling what a flight risk you are, I presume your family withdrew their offer?"

It was a slap at her elopement with his brother. She'd figured he'd work his way around to it, eventually. "No." She deliberately bit her lower lip, testing him with another ploy that rarely failed in her dealings with men. "I turned them down."

His gaze locked on her mouth once more. Male interest flashed across his face and was gone. "Why?"

He was primed for the kill. She spread her hands and went for the money shot. "To throw myself at your complete mercy, Mr. Calcagni." The beauty of it was that the trembling in her voice wasn't faked; the request she was about to make was utterly genuine. "As your sister by marriage, I am not here to debate my qualifications or lack of them. I am begging you to give me a job. I need the income. I need to be busy. I'll take whatever position you are willing to offer so long as it allows me to come to work in this particular building." She whipped her face aside, no longer able to meet his gaze. "Here," she reiterated fiercely. "Where *he* doesn't feel as far away as he does outside these walls."

Because of the number of moments it took to compose herself, she missed his initial reaction to her words. When she tipped her face up to his once more, his expression was unreadable.

"Assuming everything you say is true, Ms. Maddox, and you're not simply up to another one of your games..." He paused, his tone indicating he thought she was guilty of the latter. "We do not currently have any job openings."

"That's not what your publicist claims, and it's certainly not what you have posted on your website." She dug through her memory to resurrect a segment of the Genesis creed. "Where innovation and vision collide. Where the world's most introspective minds are ever welcome—"

"Believe me, Ms. Maddox, I am familiar with our corporate creed. There is no need to repeat it. Especially since I have already made my decision concerning your employment."

Fear sliced through her. They were only five

minutes into her interview, and he was shutting her down. "Mr. Calcagni, I—"

He stopped her with an upraised hand. "You may start your two-week trial in the morning. Eight o'clock sharp."

He was actually offering her a job? Or, in this case, a ticket to the next round? According to her inner points tally, she hadn't yet accumulated enough to win. It didn't feel like a victory, either. She had either failed to read some of his cues, or he was better at hiding them than anyone else she'd ever encountered. She no longer had any idea where they stood with each other in their banter of words, who was winning and who was losing. It made her insides weaken to the consistency of jelly.

"Since we have no vacancies in the vice presidency category," he infused an ocean-sized dose of sarcasm into his words, "you'll be serving as my personal assistant. Like every other position on our payroll, it amounts to long hours, hard work, and no coddling. You're under no obligation to accept my offer, of course."

"I accept." She couldn't contain her smile this time. She didn't understand his game, but she'd achieved what she'd come for. Employment. No matter how humble the position. Sometimes it was best not to overthink things. "Thank you, Mr. Calcagni."

There was no answering warmth in him. "You won't be thanking me tomorrow."

"A risk I will gladly take." She rose to seal her commitment with a handshake and immediately realized her mistake.

Standing brought her nearly flush with her new boss. Close enough to catch a whiff of his aftershave — a woodsy musk with a hint of cobra slithering her way. Every organ in her body suffered a tremor beneath the full blast of his scrutiny.

When his long fingers closed over hers, her insides radiated with the same intrinsic awareness of him she'd experienced nine years ago — the day they first met.

It was a complication she hadn't counted on.

<<< *To be continued...* >>>

*I hope you enjoyed this excerpt from*
**Her Billionaire Boss**
*Available in eBook and paperback on Amazon +
FREE in Kindle Unlimited!*

*Much love,*
*Jo*

THE
LAWKEEPERS

SNEAK PREVIEW: LAWFULLY LOYAL

Lilibeth Macy clenched her teeth as the small, private jet she'd chartered from New York City landed with a bouncy little bump. Though it wasn't the pilot's fault they'd had to fly through choppy winds to reach the cozy tropical town of St. Rose, she was close to tears from how much the turbulence had jarred her injuries. She was in so much pain that she debated checking into the nearest hotel and postponing her appointment with her late aunt's attorney. It was still hard to believe she'd actually inherited a beach cottage from a woman she'd never met — Jillian Ferraro, the twin sister of her estranged father, no less! As odd and unexpected as it was, the inheritance couldn't have come at a better time.

Lilibeth desperately needed a remote town in which to disappear for a few weeks while she recovered from a near-fatal car accident. No one besides her agent and tour manager knew where she was, and they were sworn to secrecy. That meant she was safe — at least for now — from the paparazzi, the endless demands of her singing career, and the constant badgering of her ex.

Her cell phone vibrated from an incoming text. She stiffened as she read it.

*Hope you made it safe to wherever you are. Call me when you can. Yours, Arlo*

Her heart thudded sickeningly, and she bit her lower lip — hard. Okay, so maybe traveling to St. Rose wouldn't stop her ex from hounding her. She briefly considered and discarded the idea of blocking his number. Knowing him as she did, he would likely use it as an excuse to come looking for her, and that was the last thing she wanted.

To an outsider, his message might sound sweetly innocuous, but she knew better. He was a controlling creep of a man who'd all but had her clock in and out with him the past year while they were dating. He'd kept tabs on every concert, charity event, and party she attended, including showing up uninvited to a few of the private ones. In short, he'd acted like he owned her, until she'd finally gotten the nerve to break things off between them two weeks ago.

The morning after their car accident.

Which he'd caused by taking the wheel while intoxicated.

He was lucky the officer on duty had recognized

her and more or less given them a free pass. He was also lucky she wasn't pressing charges against him. In some ways, she was glad he'd screwed up so badly. It had given her the perfect excuse to break up with him.

She was no longer his to text, call, or check on. Why did he persist in pretending otherwise?

Then again, Arlo Bass had never been good at taking no for an answer. He did what he wanted and took what he wanted, a trait she'd found flattering when he first started pursuing her. She'd since learned the filthy rich model and body builder was concerned about one thing only — his own needs. Their whirlwind relationship had turned toxic within the first six months. She was relieved it was over. At least, she was until a few minutes ago when he'd texted again. His inability to let go was starting to feel both suffocating and alarming. What was it going to take to send him packing for good?

Sighing, she limped her way down the short aisle of the jet. It was a sumptuous cabin of cream leather and chrome furnishings. "Thank you," she murmured to the white-haired pilot who was busy adjusting the controls in his cockpit.

He glanced up at her and smiled. "Sorry about that landing. It was pretty windy the last few minutes, wasn't it?"

"Not your fault," she assured quickly.

"Maybe not, but..." His kind gaze swept the

white plaster cast covering her left arm from elbow to wrist. "You sure you're okay?"

"I will be. Thanks." *In a few more days...or weeks...or months...* She bit her lip again and gingerly descended the stairs, one painstaking step at a time. She held the railing tightly with her right hand, silently praying she wouldn't trip. A full two weeks had passed since the accident, but her body was still recovering. Though most of her external bruises had faded, every inch of her was still stiff and sore from her many internal injuries. According to her team of doctors, she was lucky to be alive. That said, she moved around these days like a woman who was forty or fifty years older than her current twenty-five years — like a complete invalid. *Ugh!*

She reached the bottom of the stairs and filled her lungs with the fresh, tropical air. It smelled of sand, sunshine, and ocean waves. Though the June temperatures were warm and sultry, a shiver of excitement worked its way through her. She could already picture all the lazy hours she would be spending on the beach. Florida was shaping up to be the perfect place for her to convalesce in peace.

Unlike bustling tourist trap cities like Panama City and Orlando, St. Rose was apparently part of a privately owned mega resort and hotel conglomerate, located approximately one hundred miles north of Inverness. According to her late aunt's attorney, the common property and business sections of the town were managed by Montgomery Enterprises. This meant Lilibeth now owned her aunt's cottage home and about half an acre of beachfront property, but she would be responsible for paying a rather hefty set of annual resort dues to help maintain the surrounding lakes, golf courses, school, and community center. All in all, it was a small price to pay for true privacy, something that was rare and precious to a musical celebrity like herself.

Her gaze hungrily took in the small airport landing strip. About fifty yards to her left stretched the glimmering waters of the ocean. To her right was the tiny St. Rose Airport and Welcome Center. It was a white adobe building with two-story windows and a wide, covered entryway supported by enormous round pillars.

A small cargo truck, one barely bigger than a golf cart, zipped in her direction. Two employees hopped out wearing yellow and orange reflector vests. They nodded to her and proceeded to unload her significant pile of luggage. She didn't look back at them as they worked, not wanting to witness their expressions. She'd been unsure how long she would be staying in St. Rose, so she hadn't exactly packed light. There were at least a dozen suitcases and an additional four or five trunks to transport her portable amplifier, projector, expandable screen, laptop, multiple hard drives, guitar, music stand, and sheet music.

Before she had the time to shuffle her feet all the way across the parking lot to the Welcome Center, a sleek black limousine nosed alongside her and stopped. The driver, a young blonde man in a black suit, slid from behind the wheel and held up a sign bearing her name.

"Miss Lilibeth Macy?"

She nodded gratefully and waited while he opened one of the rear passenger doors for her. "Who sent you?" Normally, she was accompanied by no less than two bodyguards when she was being bustled into a limousine.

"Mr. Jack Forrest, your attorney."

As it turned out, Mr. Forrest, himself, awaited her inside the limousine. He was a short, balding man with heavily wrinkled features and a voice that held a tremor. "Ah, Miss Lilibeth! May I call you that?" He stretched out both hands to her, revealing crisp white sleeves bearing silver cufflinks beneath his herringbone blazer.

"You may." She waited until she was seated to hold out a hand.

He took it between both of his, cradling it with awe and reverence. "So we meet at last! I've heard so much about you from Jillian." He shook his head, and his dark eyes turned glassy with emotion. "May she rest in peace."

His show of emotion made Lilibeth uncomfortable, like she was intruding on something sacred. She withdrew her hand from his to fasten her seatbelt. "I'm not sure if you know this, but I never met her."

He nodded sagely, his dark gaze turning shrewd. "I am aware of that unfortunate fact."

What a presumptuous thing to say! She gaped at him. "My parents were estranged after their divorce." She'd been raised by her mother, Maureen, since age five. Her father, George Macy, had never come around — not for birthdays, holidays, music recitals, or any other events.

He nodded again. "Your parents' divorce was truly a tragic ordeal."

"He cheated on her!" Lilibeth snapped. It was unfortunate, for sure, but hardly tragic. Their short-lived marriage was a black spot in her past she quite honestly hadn't given much thought in years. She'd long since gotten over the hurt and bitterness about having an absent father. Thank God for an all-consuming career like hers. Since age fifteen, it had left her with little time for anything besides singing and performing.

Mr. Forrest shrugged the padded shoulders of his expensive suit. "I imagine you're old enough to realize there are two sides to every story." Before she could splutter out another heated response, he straightened his spine. "Here's the other side: Your Aunt Jillian loved you very much. She followed your career like it was her personal religion. Just wait until you see her collection of photos, posters, and scrapbooks. She owned every music album and every concert t-shirt. I probably ought to warn you; her home is like a shrine." He cast a sideways glance at her. "To you."

Most of the air left Lilibeth's chest. "I'm afraid I don't understand." She slumped against the black leather seat, feeling every ounce of her soreness and exhaustion.

"You will, dearie." Mr. Forrest reached over to pat the top of her right hand. "You will."

Several minutes of silence passed between them. She stared out the window. They were traveling northwest on a two-lane highway that overlooked the beach. Here and there, a beachcomber lay sunning or a small cluster of people in swimsuits played beach ball, but the area was otherwise free of traffic and the usual throng of humans. On either side of the road were well-manicured medians bearing palm trees and plants with fiery tropical blooms.

Lilibeth turned abruptly to face Jack Forrest. "What happened to my aunt? At least tell me that."

He offered her a sad smile. "Lung cancer, I'm afraid. She was a closet smoker. Her only vice, from what I could tell."

"And her husband?" Her aunt's last name was Ferraro, which meant she had to have married at some point.

"Taken from her by a blasted heart attack a few years back." He grimaced and patted her hand again.

"No children, though they always wanted them. In some ways, you were like the daughter they never had."

"How?" Lilibeth couldn't quite get her arms around such a preposterous claim. "Like I said before, we never met."

He grinned as if laughing at a private joke. "You did hear the part about her owning every concert t-shirt of yours, right?"

Her brows shot up. "You're trying to tell me my aunt, whom I never met, attended my concerts?"

"Every single one." His emphatic nod nearly brought his chin to his chest.

Her throat constricted as she struggled to understand. "Why didn't she reach out to me? I would have..." She stopped short, not knowing what she would have done if she had known her aunt was in the audience at one of her concerts. Ever since she could remember, her mother had forbidden her to have any contact with the Macy side of the family.

"She tried. See?" Jack Forrest spread his hands as the limousine slowed and pulled into a residential neighborhood. "Like I said, there are two sides to every story."

"Why am I just now hearing about this?" Lilibeth demanded irritably.

"Your mother refused to let them contact you, claiming they had no right to disrupt your life and musical career with more of their so-called family drama."

"Oh-h-h-h." Her breath came out slowly, drawing out the word. That sure sounded like something Maureen Macy would say. She'd always been a helicopter parent — hovering over every bite that went into her daughter's mouth, personally selecting nearly every outfit she wore, and micromanaging her voice and guitar practice schedules.

Lilibeth hadn't enjoyed a normal childhood by any stretch. There'd been precious few outings with other children her age, since her mother insisted that perfecting her craft was far more important than playing. And there'd been zero contact with George Macy or anyone else on his side of the family. Lilibeth had always presumed it was because her father didn't want anything to do with her. Was it possible there was another reason?

"Have you met my father? Do you know anything about him? Where he lives? What he does for a living?" The questions poured from her like a dam bursting.

The limousine driver braked and brought the vehicle to a halt.

"We're here!" Jack Forrest announced. "This is the home Jillian Ferraro left to you, her beloved niece."

The increased cadence of his words gave her the

impression he was relieved to have an excuse not to immediately answer her questions about her father.

She gazed out the door their driver opened for her, and her mouth fell open. Her brain had conjured up all sorts of images on the plane ride to St. Rose, but nothing prepared her for the Mediterranean style mansion sprawling before her. A vast swimming pool with a lazy river circled one side of the property beneath waving palms. A two-story cottage graced the other side, boasting the same Mediterranean lines as the mansion. It was simply a lot smaller. Sort of... It was still a two-story in its own right, but it was more or less dwarfed by the enormous structure next door.

*I was told my aunt left me her beach cottage.* Lilibeth's gaze drifted back to the smaller home. She pointed to it. "Is that one mine?"

"All yours, love," he assured with his cheerful tremor.

"And the mansion next door?" She was sort of dying to know who her neighbors were.

"The Montgomerys. They own the resort, well, pretty much the whole town." His tone was offhand as if it was no big deal. "Oh, hey!" He raised a hand, gnarled with arthritis, to wave at a dark-haired man swimming in their direction. "There's ol' Chuck's grandson, Barrett. Thought I heard he was back in town."

*Oh, no!* Lilibeth's uninjured hand flew automatically to her hair. She really, really, really did *not* feel up to meeting another rich playboy, but it didn't sound like she was going to be given a choice. She hastily finger-combed her cascade of long, dark hair back from her face and cast a critical eye down at her hot pink sundress. It would have to do. There was no time to change. *Shoot!* She'd completely forgotten to make arrangements to have her luggage delivered from the airport.

Her bleat of alarm made Jack Forrest return his attentions to her. "Is everything alright, Lilibeth?"

"Not exactly." She grimaced at him. "I forgot all about my luggage."

"But I didn't." He held up a finger and grinned at her. "A shuttle van will be on its way shortly with your things."

"Oh, my goodness!" she sighed in relief. "You wonderful man! I could totally kiss you right now."

Still grinning, the wily fellow actually sidled closer and tipped up his heavily lined face to hers.

In the same moment, a tall Roman god of a man rose from the swimming pool with water streaming down his sun-kissed chest and arms. He raised one dark brow at them. "Am I interrupting something?"

<<< *To be continued...* >>>

*I hope you enjoyed this excerpt from*
**THE LAWKEEPERS:**

## **Lawfully Loyal**

*Available now in eBook and paperback on Amazon + FREE in Kindle Unlimited!*

*Much love,*
*Jo*

Jo is an Amazon bestselling author of sweet and inspirational romance stories with humor, heart, and happily-ever-afters.

## Free Book!

Visit www.JoGrafford.com to sign up for Jo's New Release Newsletter and receive a FREE copy of a festive short story — **Lawfully Courageous**.

**1.) Follow on Amazon!**
amazon.com/author/jografford

**2.) Join Cuppa Jo Readers!**

https://www.facebook.com/
groups/CuppaJoReaders

### 3.) Join Heroes and Hunks Readers!
https://www.facebook.com/
groups/HeroesandHunks/

### 4.) Follow on Bookbub!
https://www.bookbub.com/authors/jo-grafford

### 5.) Follow on Instagram!
https://www.instagram.com/jografford/

amazon.com/authors/jo-grafford

bookbub.com/authors/jo-grafford

facebook.com/jografford

twitter.com/jografford

instagram.com/jografford

pinterest.com/jografford

*a multi-author series*

Elizabeth

Grace

-----

**Once Upon a Church House Series**

*written exclusively by Jo Grafford*

Abigail

Rachel

Naomi

-----

**Black Tie Billionaires**

*written exclusively by Jo Grafford*

Her Billionaire Boss

Her Billionaire Bodyguard

Her Billionaire Secret Admirer

Her Billionaire Best Friend

-----

**The Lawkeepers**

*a multi-author series*

Lawfully Ours

Lawfully Loyal

Lawfully Witnessed

Lawfully Brave

Lawfully Courageous

-----

**Disaster City Search and Rescue**

*a multi-author series*

The Rebound Rescue

The Plus One Rescue

The Blind Date Rescue

The Fake Bride Rescue

The Secret Baby Rescue

-----

**Border Brides**

*a multi-author Series*

Wild Rose Summer

Going All In

-----

**Billionaire's Birthday Club**

*a multi-author series*

The Billionaire's Birthday Date

-----

## The Pinkerton Matchmaker

### *a multi-author series*

An Agent for Bernadette

An Agent for Lorelai

An Agent for Jolene

An Agent for Madeleine

-----

## Lost Colony Series

### *written exclusively by Jo Grafford*

Breaking Ties

Trail of Crosses

Into the Mainland

Higher Tides

-----

## Ornamental Match Maker Series

### *a multi-author series*

Angel Cookie Christmas

Star-Studded Christmas

Stolen Heart Valentine

Miracle for Christmas in July

Home for Christmas

_____

**Whispers In Wyoming**

*a multi-author series*

His Wish, Her Command

His Heart, Her Love

_____

**Silverpines**

*a multi-author series*

Wanted: Bounty Hunter

The Bounty Hunter's Sister

_____

**The Bride Herder**

*a multi-author series*

Herd the Heavens

_____

**Brides of Pelican Rapids**

*a multi-author series*

Rebecca's Dream

-----

**Sailors and Saints**

*a multi-author series*

The Sailor and the Surgeon

Made in the USA
Middletown, DE
21 June 2021